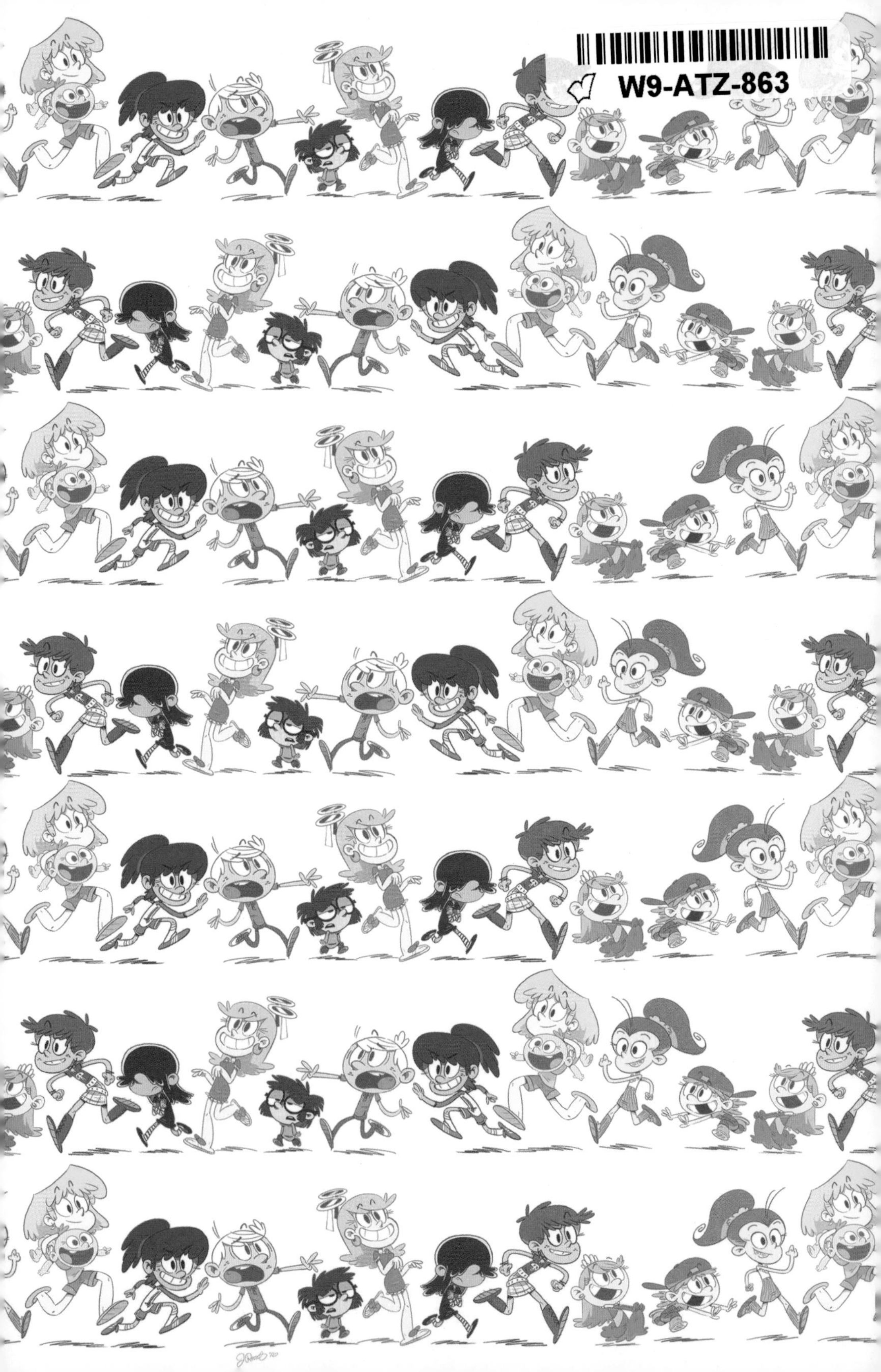

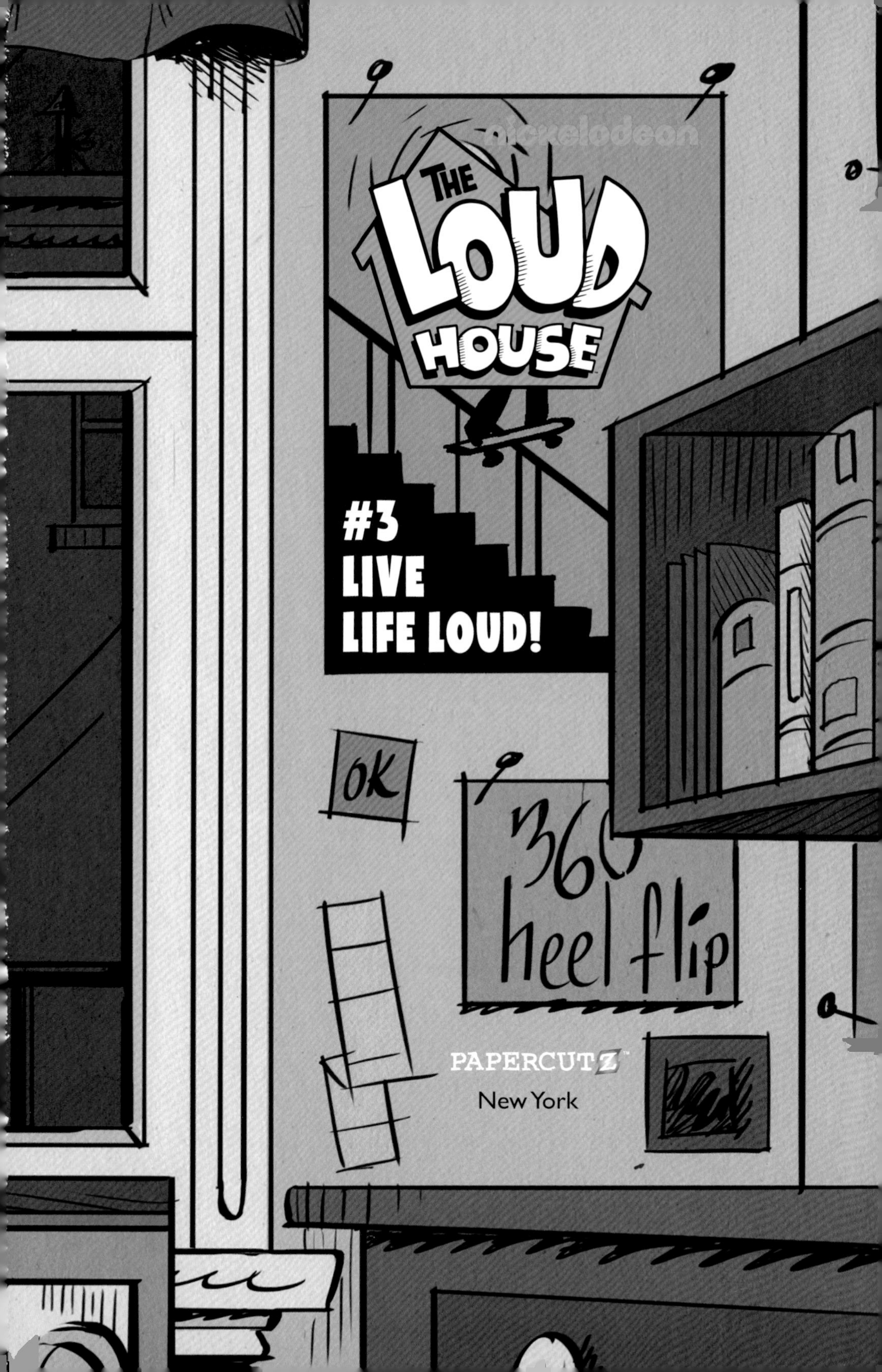
nickelodeon
THE LOUD HOUSE
#3
LIVE
LIFE LOUD!
OK
360 heel flip

PAPERCUTZ
New York

NICKELODEON GRAPHIC NOVELS AVAILABLE FROM PAPERCUTZ

THESE ALSO INCLUDE LOUD HOUSE STORIES!

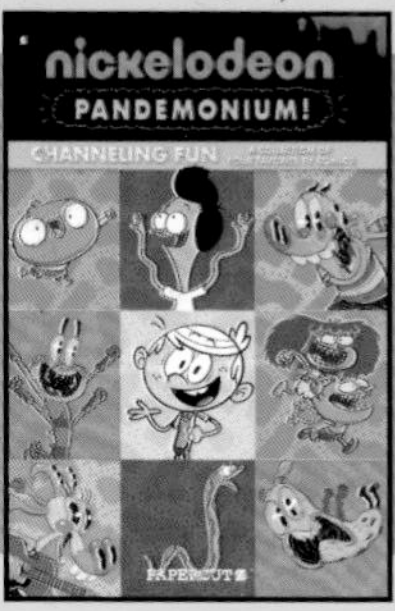
nickelodeon
PANDEMONIUM!
CHANNELING FUN
PAPERCUTZ

NICKELODEON PANDEMONIUM #1 "Channeling Fun"

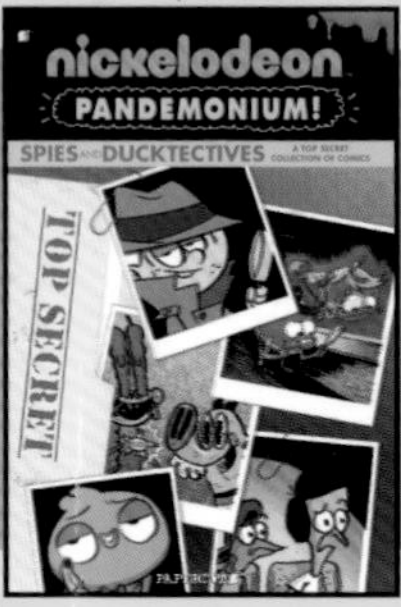
nickelodeon
PANDEMONIUM!
SPIES AND DUCKTECTIVES
TOP SECRET

NICKELODEON PANDEMONIUM #2 "Spies and Ducktectives"

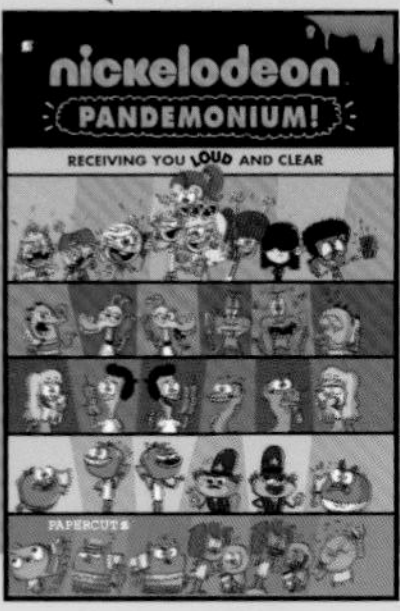
nickelodeon
PANDEMONIUM!
RECEIVING YOU LOUD AND CLEAR
PAPERCUTZ

NICKELODEON PANDEMONIUM #3 "Receiving You Loud and Clear"

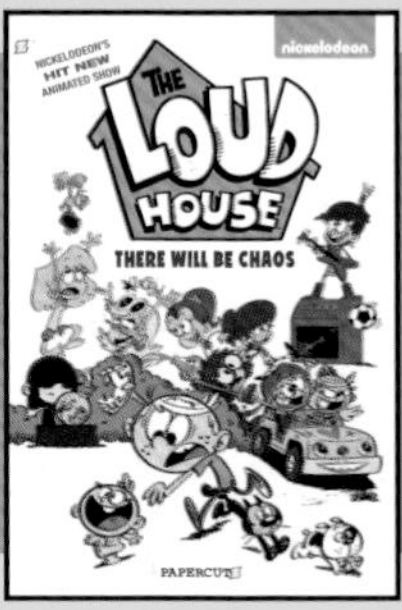
nickelodeon
THE LOUD HOUSE
THERE WILL BE CHAOS
PAPERCUTZ

THE LOUD HOUSE #1 "There Will Be Chaos"

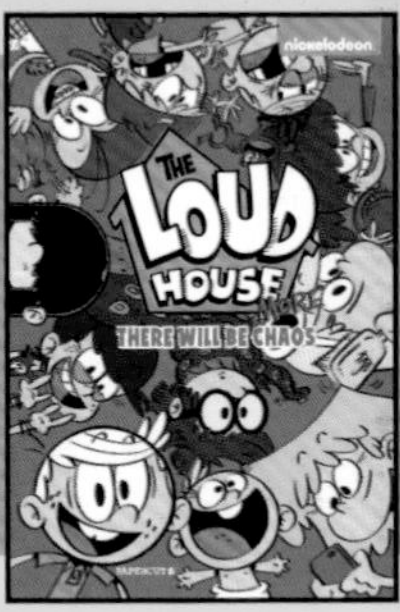
nickelodeon
THE LOUD HOUSE
THERE WILL BE CHAOS
PAPERCUTZ

THE LOUD HOUSE #2 "There Will Be More Chaos"

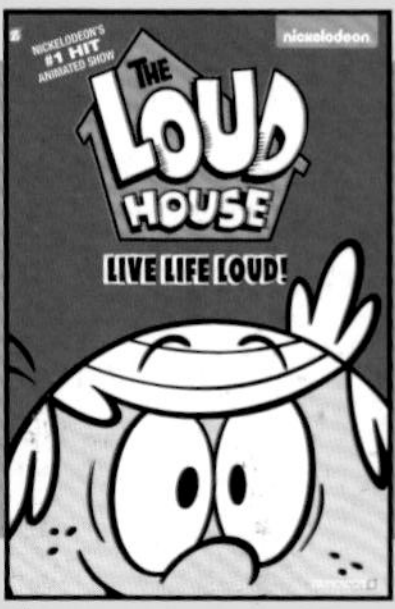
nickelodeon
THE LOUD HOUSE
LIVE LIFE LOUD!

THE LOUD HOUSE #3 "Live Life Loud!"

COMING SOON!

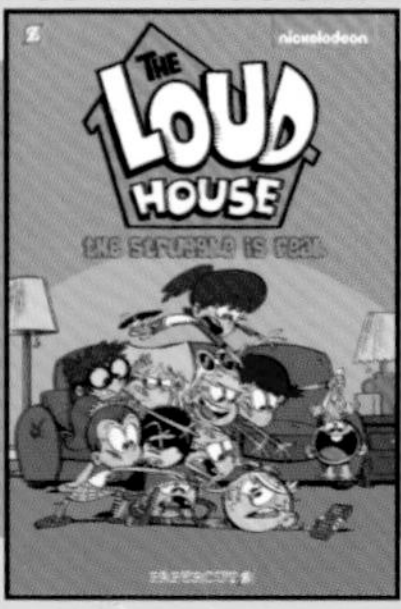
nickelodeon
THE LOUD HOUSE
PAPERCUTZ

THE LOUD HOUSE #4 "The Struggle is Real"

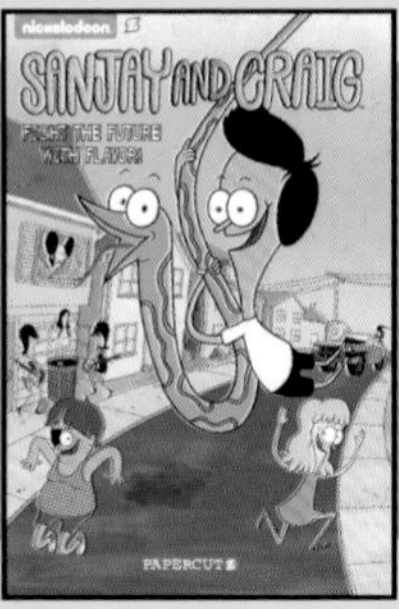
nickelodeon
SANJAY AND CRAIG
PAPERCUTZ

SANJAY AND CRAIG #1 "Fight the Future with Flavor"

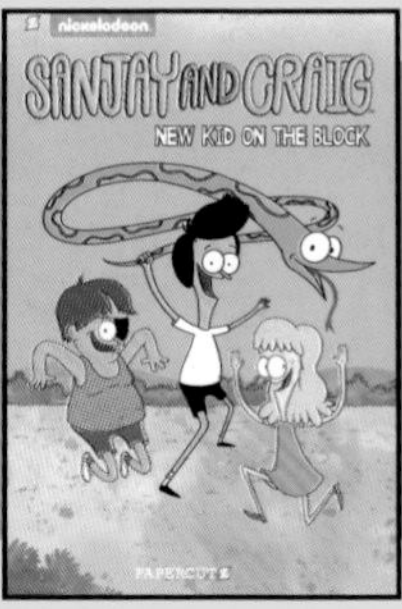
nickelodeon
SANJAY AND CRAIG
NEW KID ON THE BLOCK
PAPERCUTZ

SANJAY AND CRAIG #2 "New Kid on the Block"

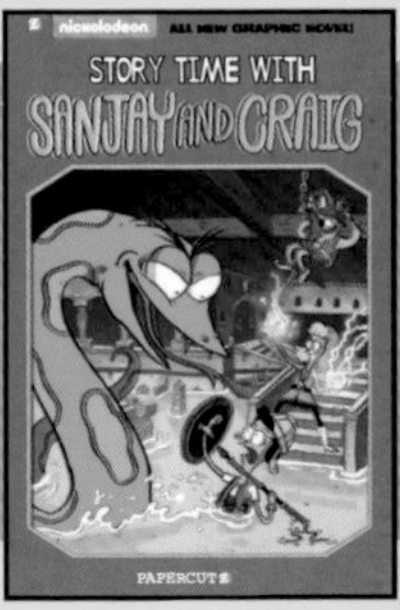
nickelodeon
STORY TIME WITH
SANJAY AND CRAIG
PAPERCUTZ

SANJAY AND CRAIG #3 "Story Time with Sanjay and Craig"

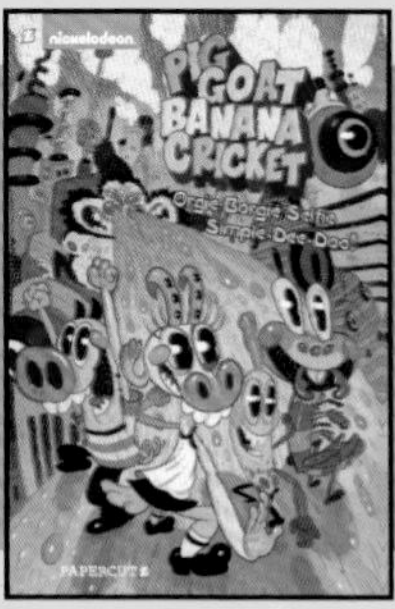
nickelodeon
PIG GOAT BANANA CRICKET
PAPERCUTZ

PIG GOAT BANANA CRICKET #1 "Orgle Borgle Selfie Simple-Dee Doo!"

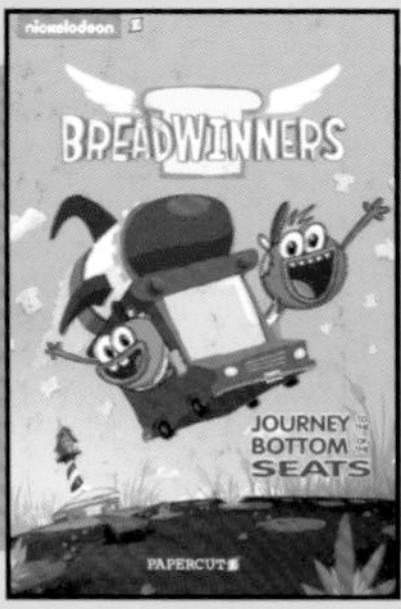
nickelodeon
BREADWINNERS
JOURNEY
BOTTOM
SEATS
PAPERCUTZ

BREADWINNERS #1 "Journey to the Bottom of the Seats"

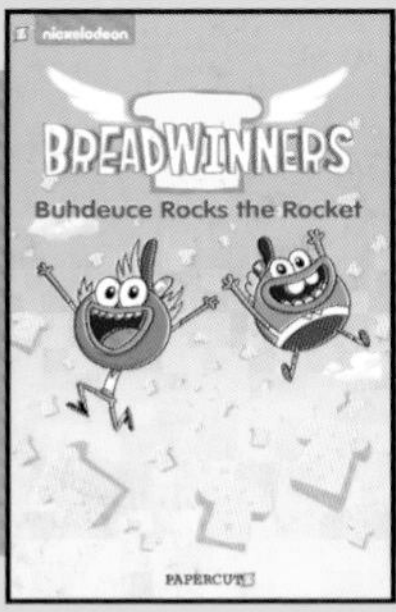
nickelodeon
BREADWINNERS
Buhdeuce Rocks the Rocket
PAPERCUTZ

BREADWINNERS #2 "Buhdeuce Rocks the Rocket"

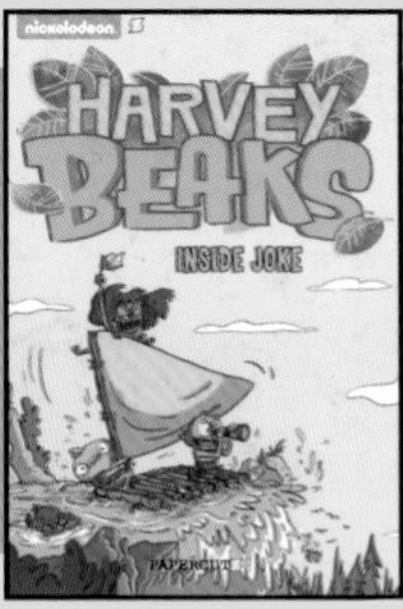
nickelodeon
HARVEY BEAKS
INSIDE JOKE
PAPERCUTZ

HARVEY BEAKS #1 "Inside Joke"

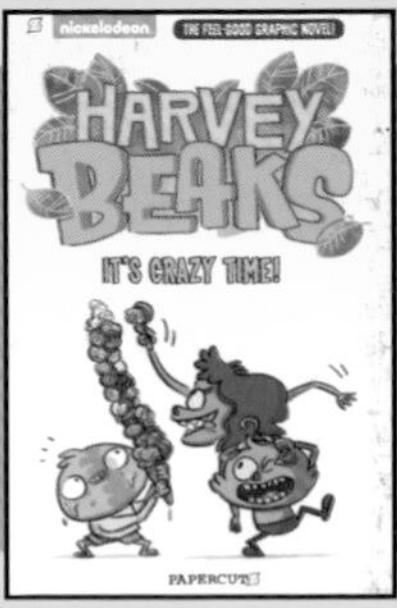
nickelodeon
HARVEY BEAKS
IT'S CRAZY TIME!
PAPERCUTZ

HARVEY BEAKS #2 "It's Crazy Time"

Nickelodeon graphic novels are available for $7.99 each in paperback, $12.99 each in hardcover. NICKELODEON PANDEMINIUM #3 is $8.99 each in paperback, $13.99 each in hardcover. Available from booksellers everywhere. You can also order online from Papercutz.com, or call 1-800-886-1223, Monday through Friday, 9-5 EST. MC, Visa, and AmEx accepted. To order by mail, please add $5.00 for postage and handling for the first book ordered, $1.00 for each additional book and make check payable to NBM Publishing. Send to: Papercutz, 160 Broadway, Suite 700, East Wing, New York, NY 10038.

THE LOUD HOUSE

#3 LIVE LIFE LOUD!

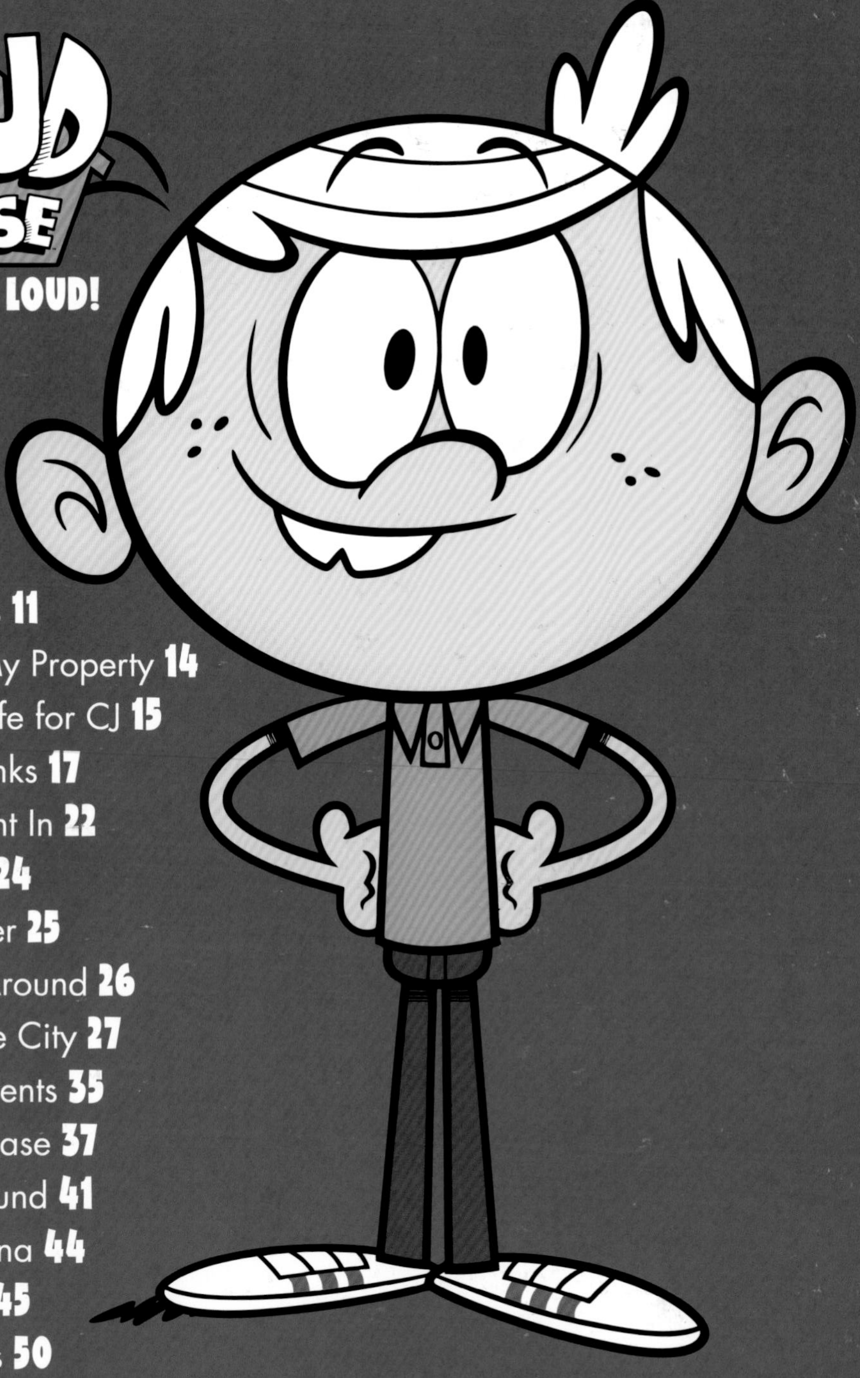

nickelodeon™ THE LOUD HOUSE

#3 "LIVE LIFE LOUD!"

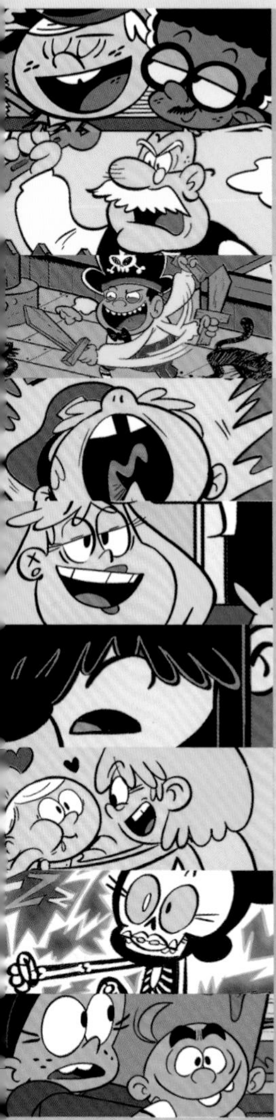

"PRIVATE EYES"
Jordan Koch
Writer, Artist, Letterer, Colorist

"PACKING PARENTS"
Jordan Koch
Writer, Artist, Letterer, Colorist

"MY YARD, MY PROPERTY"
Jared Morgan
Writer, Artist, Letterer, Colorist

"IT'S JUST A PHASE"
Miguel Puga–Writer, Artist, Letterer
Ashley Kliment–Colorist

"A PIRATE'S LIFE FOR CJ"
Whitney Wetta—Writer
Jared Morgan—Artist, Letterer, Colorist

"LOST AND FOUND"
Diem Doan
Writer, Artist, Letterer, Colorist

"HICCUP HIJINKS"
Sammie Crowley—Writer
Ari Castleton—Artist, Letterer
Ashley Kliment—Colorist

"I SPY LASAGNA"
Diem Doan
Writer, Artist, Letterer, Colorist

"MOM'S NIGHT IN"
Whitney Wetta—Writer
Jordan Rosato—Artist, Letterer
Diem Doan—Colorist

"SAM'S PICK"
Kevin Sullivan—Writer
Jordan Koch—Artist, Letterer, Colorist

"GOTH PERKS"
Miguel Puga—Writer, Artist, Letterer
Diem Doan—Colorist

"SHARE BEARS"
Whitney Wetta—Writer
Erin Hyde—Artist, Letterer
Diem Doan–Colorist

"BABY BROTHER"
Diem Doan
Writer, Artist, Letterer, Colorist

"HELP WANTED"
Jared Morgan
Writer, Artist, Letterer, Colorist

"CLOWNING AROUND"
Whitney Wetta—Writer
Jordan Rosato—Artist, Letterer
Diem Doan—Colorist

"ABCs OF GETTING THE LAST SLICE"
Chris Savino—Writer, Artist
Jordan Rosato—Artist, Letterer
Amanda Rynda—Colorist

"BABES IN THE CITY"
Sammie Crowley & Whitney Wetta—Writers
Ida Hem—Artist, Colorist, Letterer

"BEDTIME STORIES"
Jared Morgan
Writer, Artist, Letterer, Colorist

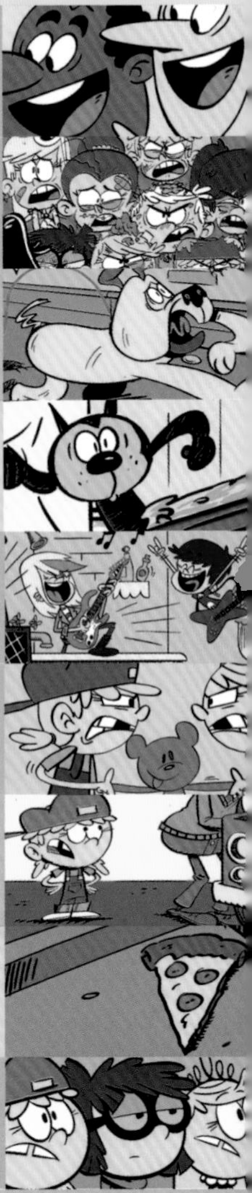

CHRIS SAVINO—Cover Artist
JORDAN ROSATO—Endpapers
JAMES SALERNO—Sr. Art Director/Nickelodeon
DAWN GUZZO—Design
SEAN GANTKA—Special Thanks
SPENSER NELLIS—Editorial Intern
JEFF WHITMAN—Editor
JOAN HILTY—Comics Editor/Nickelodeon
JIM SALICRUP
Editor-in-Chief

ISBN: 978-1-62991-863-1 paperback edition
ISBN: 978-1-62991-862-4 hardcover edition

Papercutz books may be purchased for business or promotional use. For information on bulk purchases please contact Macmillan Corporate and Premium Sales Department at (800) 221-7945 x5442.

Printed in China
March 2018

Distributed by Macmillan
First Printing

MEET THE LOUD FAMILY *and friends!*

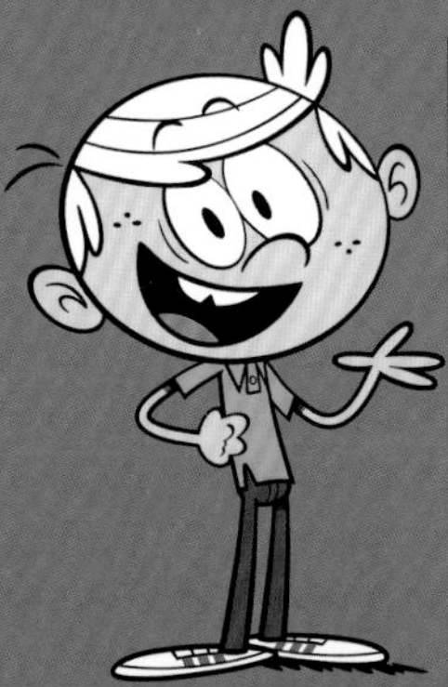

LINCOLN LOUD
THE MIDDLE CHILD (11)

At 11 years old, Lincoln is the middle child, with five older sisters and five younger sisters. He has learned that surviving the Loud household means staying a step ahead. He's the man with a plan, always coming up with a way to get what he wants or deal with a problem, even if things inevitably go wrong. Being the only boy comes with some perks. Lincoln gets his own room – even if it's just a converted linen closet. On the other hand, being the only boy also means he sometimes gets a little too much attention from his sisters. They mother him, tease him, and use him as the occasional lab rat or fashion show participant. Lincoln's sisters may drive him crazy, but he loves them and is always willing to help out if they need him.

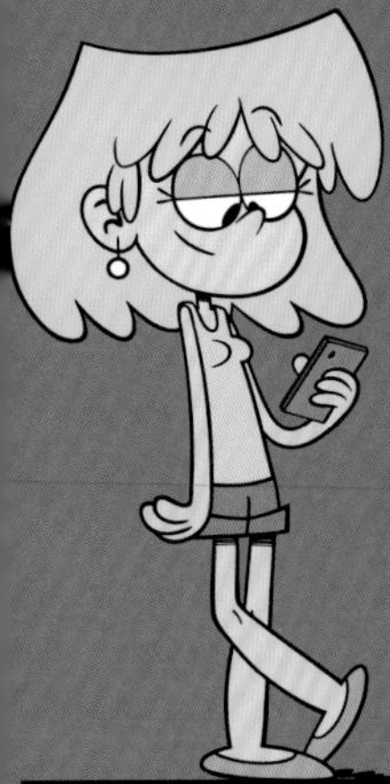

LORI LOUD
THE OLDEST (17)

As the first-born child of the Loud clan, Lori sees herself as the boss of all her siblings. She feels she's paved the way for them and deserves extra respect. Her signature traits are rolling her eyes, texting her boyfriend Bobby, and literally saying "literally" all the time. Because she's the oldest and most experienced sibling, Lori can be a great ally, so it pays to stay on her good side.

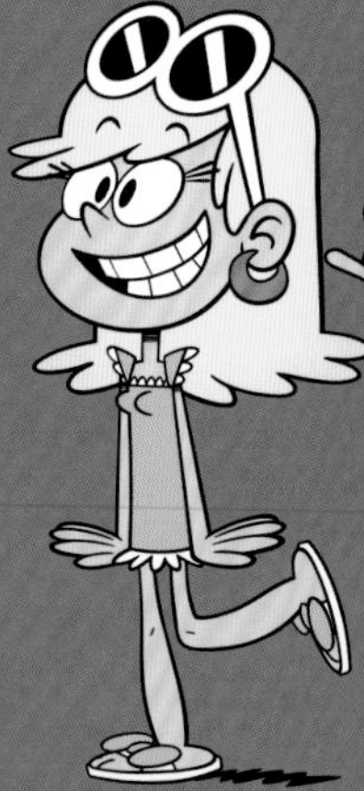

LENI LOUD
THE FASHIONISTA (16)

Leni spends most of her time designing outfits and accessorizing. She always falls for Luan's pranks, and sometimes walks into walls when she's talking (she's not great at doing two things at once). Leni might be flighty, but she's the sweetest of the Loud siblings and truly has a heart of gold (even though she's pretty sure it's a heart of blood).

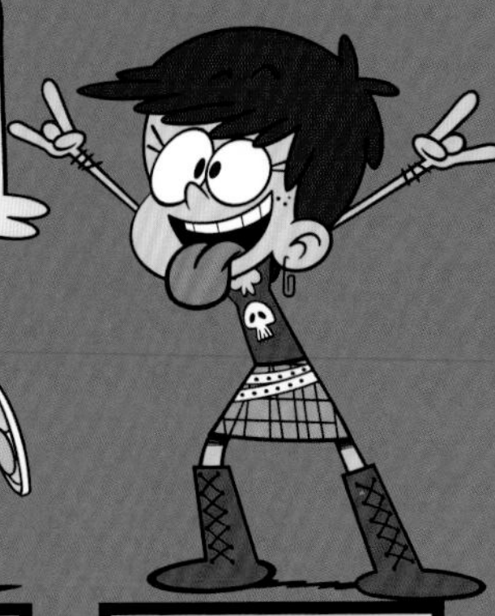

LUNA LOUD
THE ROCK STAR (15)

Luna is loud, boisterous and freewheeling, and her energy is always cranked to 11. She thinks about music so much that she even talks in song lyrics. On the off-chance she doesn't have her guitar with her, everything can and will be turned into a musical instrument. You can always count on Luna to help out, and she'll do most anything you ask, as long as you're okay with her supplying a rocking guitar accompaniment.

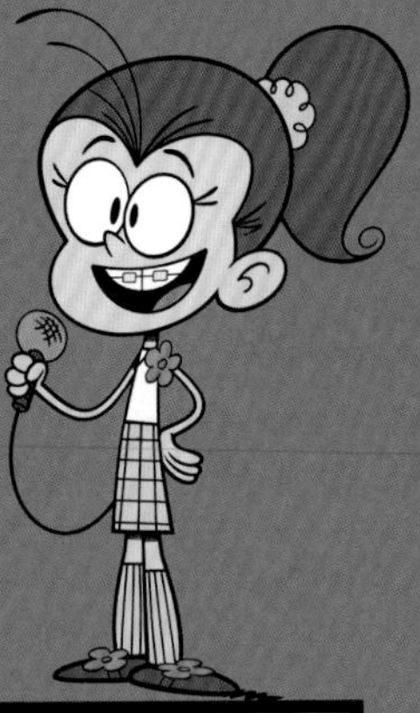

LUAN LOUD
THE JOKESTER (14)

Luan's a standup comedienne who provides a nonstop barrage of silly puns. She's big on prop comedy too – squirting flowers and whoopee cushions – so you have to be on your toes whenever she's around. She loves to pull pranks and is a really good ventriloquist – she is often found doing bits with her dummy, Mr. Coconuts. Luan never lets anything get her down; to her, laughter IS the best medicine.

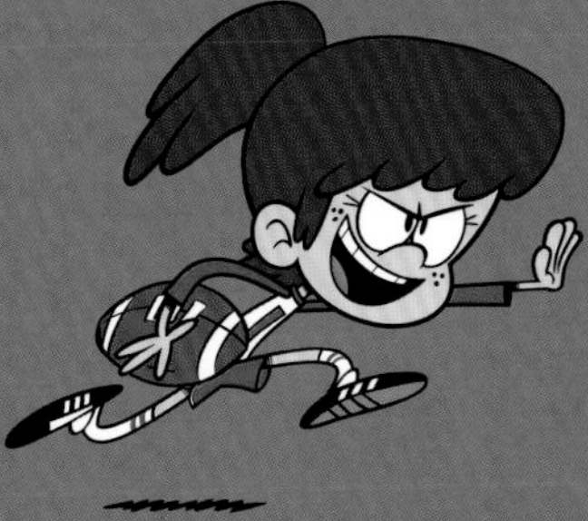

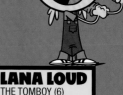

LYNN LOUD
THE ATHLETE (13)

Lynn is athletic and full of energy and is always looking for a teammate. With her, it's all sports all the time. She'll turn anything into a sport. Putting away eggs? Jump shot! Score! Cleaning up the eggs? Slap shot! Score! Lynn is very competitive, tends to be superstitious about her teams, and accepts almost any dare.

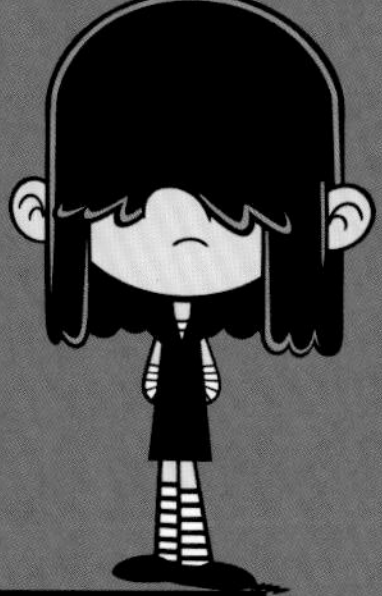

LUCY LOUD
THE EMO (8)

You can always count on Lucy to give the morbid point of view in any given situation. She is obsessed with all things spooky and dark – funerals, vampires, séances, and the like. She wears mostly black and writes moody poetry. She's usually quiet and keeps to herself. Lucy has a way of mysteriously appearing out of nowhere, and try as they might, her siblings never get used to this.

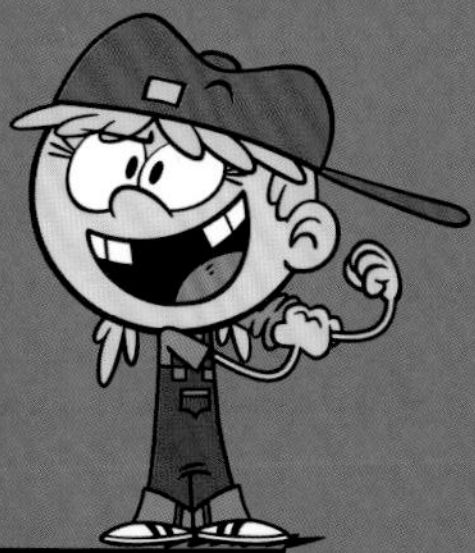

LANA LOUD
THE TOMBOY (6)

Lana is the rough-and-tumble sparkplug counterpart to her twin sister, Lola. She's all about reptiles, mud pies, and muffler repair. She's the resident Ms. Fix-it and is always ready to lend a hand – the dirtier the job, the better. Need your toilet unclogged? Snake fed? Back-zit popped? Lana's your gal. All she asks in return is a little A-B-C gum, or a handful of kibble (she often sneaks it from the dog bowl).

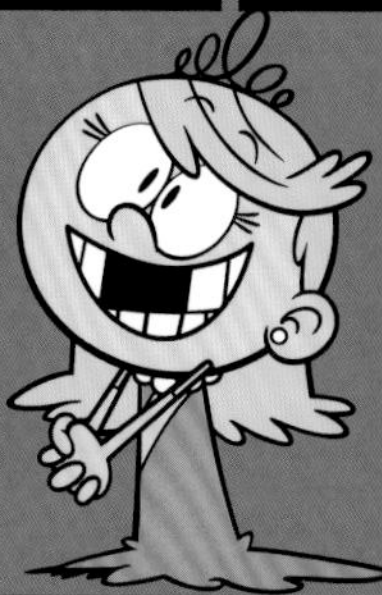

LOLA LOUD
THE BEAUTY QUEEN (6)

Lola could not be more different from her twin sister, Lana. She's a pageant powerhouse whose interests include glitter, photo shoots, and her own beautiful, beautiful face. But don't let her cute, gap-toothed smile fool you; underneath all the sugar and spice lurks a Machiavellian mastermind. Whatever Lola wants, Lola gets – or else. She's the eyes and ears of the household and never resists an opportunity to tattle on troublemakers. But if you stay on Lola's good side, you've got yourself a fierce ally – and a lifetime supply of free makeovers.

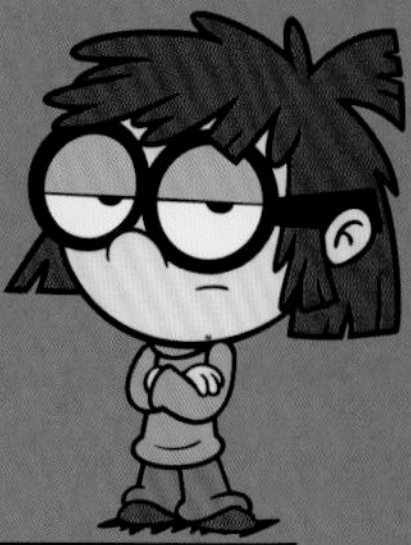

LISA LOUD
THE GENIUS (4)

Lisa is smarter than the rest of her siblings combined. She'll most likely be a rocket scientist, or a brain surgeon, or an evil genius who takes over the world. Lisa spends most of her time working in her lab (the family has gotten used to the explosions), and says her research leaves little time for frivolous human pursuits like "playing" or "getting haircuts." That said, she's always there to help with a homework question, or to explain why the sky is blue, or to point out the structural flaws in someone's pillow fort. Lisa says it's the least she can do for her favorite test subjects, er, siblings.

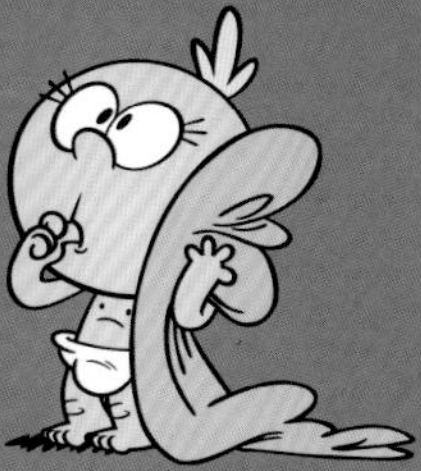

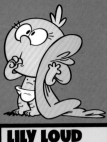

LILY LOUD
THE BABY (15 MONTHS)

Lily is a giggly, drooly, diaper-ditching free spirit, affectionately known as "the poop machine." You can't keep a nappy on this kid – she's like a teething Houdini. But even when Lily's running wild, dropping rancid diaper bombs, or drooling all over the remote, she always brings a smile to everyone's face (and a clothespin to their nose). Lily is everyone's favorite little buddy, and the whole family loves her unconditionally.

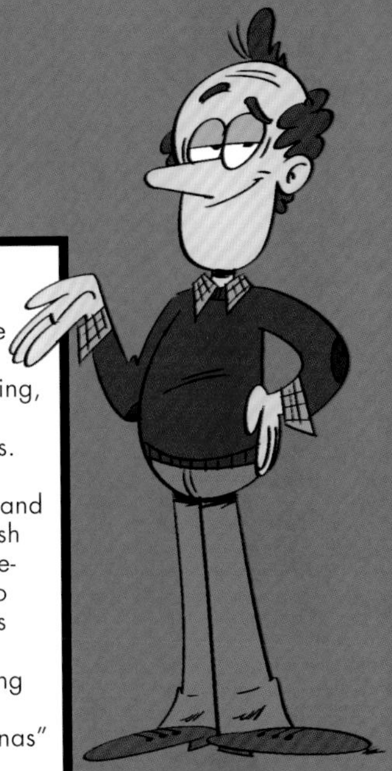

LYNN LOUD SR.

Dad (Lynn Loud Sr.) is a fun-loving, upbeat aspiring chef. A kid-at-heart, he's not above taking part in the kids' zany schemes. In addition to cooking, Dad loves his van, playing the cowbell and making puns. Before meeting Mom, Dad spent a semester in England and has been obsessed with British culture ever since – and sometimes "accidentally" slips into a British accent. When Dad's not wrangling the kids, he's pursuing his dream of opening his own restaurant where he hopes to make his "Lynn-sagnas" world famous.

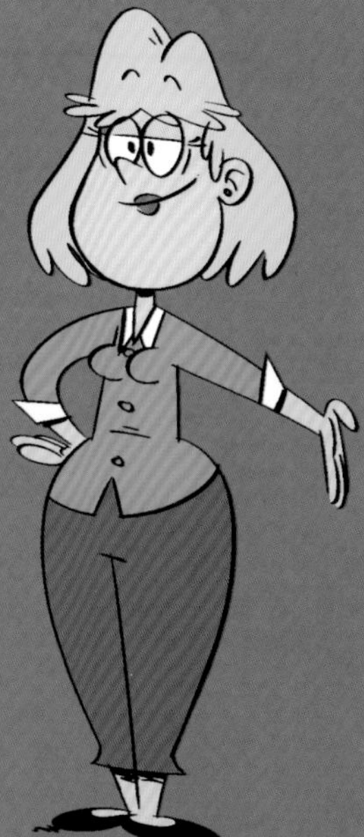

RITA LOUD

Mother to the eleven Loud kids, Mom (Rita Loud) wears many different hats. She's a chauffeur, homework-checker and barf-cleaner-upper all rolled into one. She's always there for her kids and ready to jump into action during a crisis, whether it's a fight between the twins or Leni's missing shoe. When she's not chasing the kids around or at her day job as a dental hygienist, Mom pursues her passion: writing. She also loves taking on house projects and is very handy with tools (guess that's where Lana gets it from). Between writing, working and being a mom, her days are always hectic but she wouldn't have it any other way.

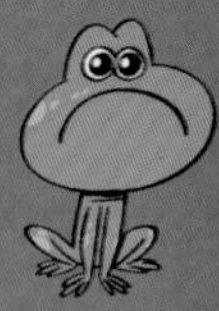

HOPS

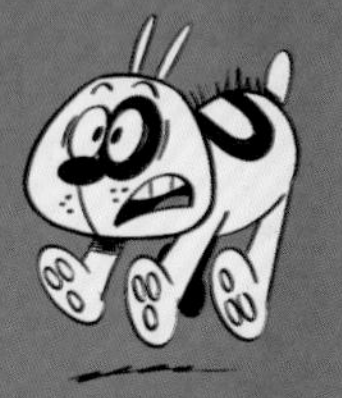

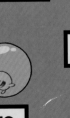

CHARLES

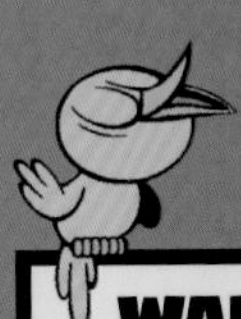

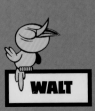

WALT

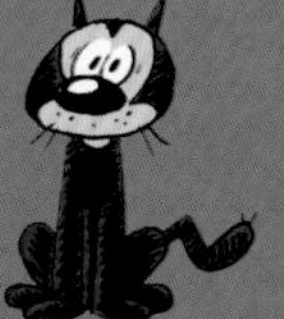

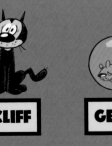

CLIFF

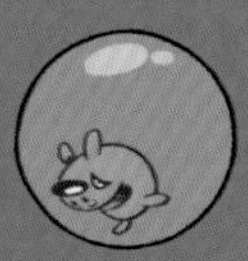

GEO

RONNIE ANNE SANTIAGO

Ronnie Anne's an independent spirit who's into skating, gaming and pranking. Strong-willed and a little gruff, she isn't into excessive displays of emotion. But don't be fooled – she has a sweet side, too, fostered by years of taking care of her mother and brother. And though her new extended family can be a little overwhelming, she appreciates how loving, caring and fun they can be.

BOBBY SANTIAGO

Ronnie Anne's older brother, Bobby is a sweet, responsible, loyal high-school senior who works in the family's bodega. Bobby is very devoted to his family. He's Grandpa's right hand man and can't wait to one day take over the bodega for him. Bobby's a big kid and a bit of a klutz, which sometimes gets him into pickles, like locking himself in the freezer case. But he makes up for any work mishaps with his great customer skills – everyone in the neighborhood loves him.

MARIA CASAGRANDE SANTIAGO

She's the mother of Bobby and Ronnie Anne. A hardworking nurse, she doesn't get to spend a lot of time with her kids, but when she does, she treasures it. Maria is calm and rational but often worries about whether she's doing enough for her kids. Maria, Bobby, and Ronnie Anne are a close-knit trio who were used to having only each other – until they moved in with their extended family.

HECTOR CASAGRANDE

He's the father of Carlos and Maria and the grandfather of six. The patriarch of the Casagrande Family, Hector wears the pants (or at least thinks he does). He is the owner of the bodega on the ground floor of their apartment building and takes great pride in his work, his family, and being the unofficial "mayor" of the block. He's charismatic, friendly, and also a huge gossip (although he tries to deny it).

ROSA CASAGRANDE

She's the mother of Carlos and Maria and wife to Hector. Rosa is a gifted cook and has a sixth sense about knowing when anyone in her house is hungry. The wisest of the bunch, Rosa is really the head of the household but lets Hector think he is. She's spiritual and often tries to fix problems or illnesses with home remedies or potions. She's protective of all her family, and at times can be a bit smothering.

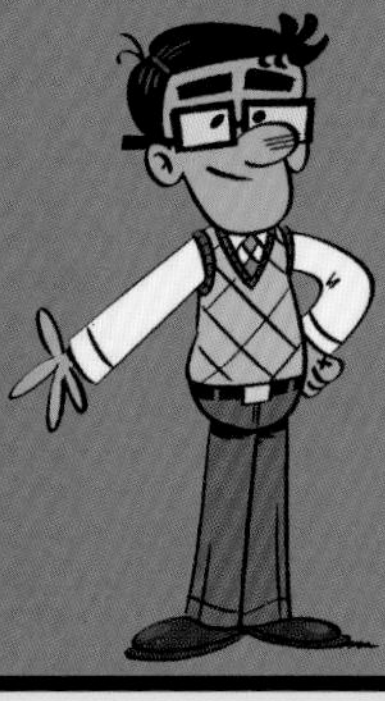

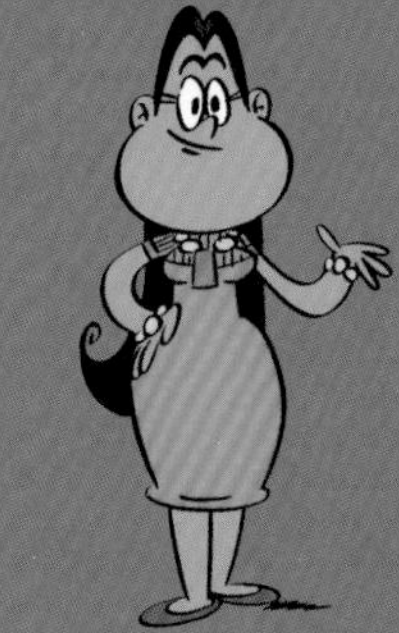

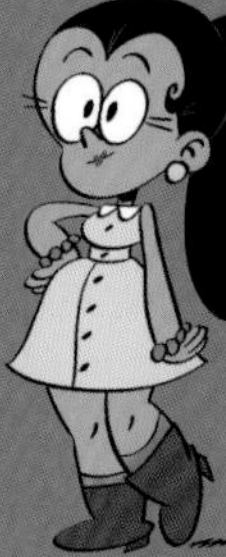

CARLOS CASAGRANDE

He's the father of four kids (Carlota, CJ, Carl, and Carlitos), husband of Frida and brother of Maria. He's a professor of marine biology at a local college and always has his head in a book. He's a pretty easygoing guy compared to his sometimes overly emotional relatives. Carlos is pragmatic, a caring father and loves to rattle off useless tidbits of information.

FRIDA PUGA CASAGRANDE

She's the mother to Carlota, CJ, Carl, and Carlitos and wife to Carlos. She's an artist-type, always taking photos of the family. She tends to cry when she's overcome with sadness, anger, happiness... basically, she cries a lot. She's excitable, game for fun, passionate, and loves her family more than anything. All she ever wants is for her entire family to be in the same room. But when that happens, all she can do is cry and take photos.

CARLOTA CASAGRANDE

The oldest child of Carlos and Frida. She's social, fun-loving, and desperately wants to be the big sister to Ronnie Anne. Carlota has a very distinctive vintage style, which she tries to share with Ronnie Anne, who couldn't be less interested.

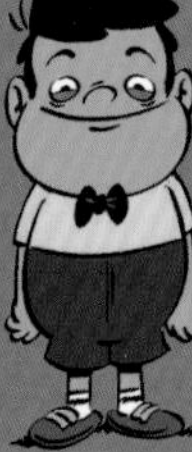

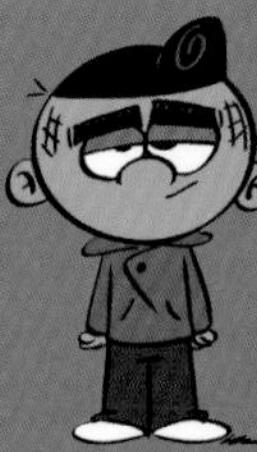

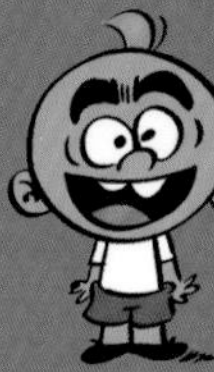

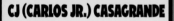

CJ (CARLOS JR.) CASAGRANDE

CJ was born with Down syndrome. He's the sunshine in everyone's life and always wants to play. He will often lighten the mood of a tense situation with his honest remarks. He adores Bobby and always wants to be around him (which is A-OK with Bobby, who sees CJ as a little brother). CJ asks to wear a bowtie every day no matter the occasion and is hardly ever without a smile on his face. He's definitely a glass-half-full kind of guy.

CARL CASAGRANDE

Carlino is 6 going on 30. He thinks of himself as a suave, romantic ladies' man. He's confident and out-going. When he sees something he likes, he goes for it (even if it's Bobby's girlfriend, Lori). He cares about his appearance even more than Carlota and often uses her hair products (much to her chagrin). He hates to be reminded that he's only six and is emasculated whenever someone notices him snuggling his blankie or sucking his thumb. Carl is convinced that Bobby is his biggest rival and is always trying to beat Bobby (which Bobby is unaware of).

CARLITOS CASAGRANDE

The red-headed toddler who is always mimicking everyone's behavior, even the dog's. He's playful, rambunctious and loves to play with the family pets.

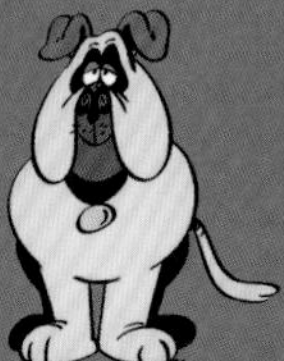

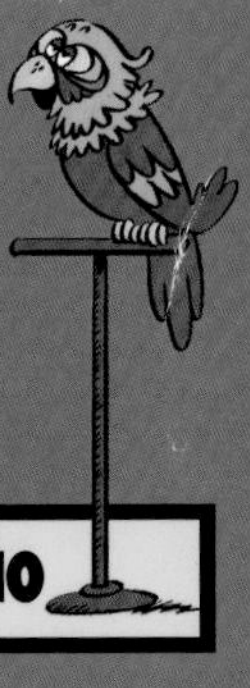

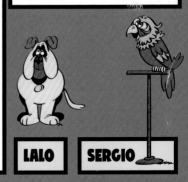

LALO

SERGIO

CLYDE McBRIDE
THE BEST FRIEND (11)

Clyde is Lincoln's partner in crime. He's always willing to go along with Lincoln's crazy schemes (even if he sees the flaws in them up front). Lincoln and Clyde are two peas in a pod and share pretty much all of the same tastes in movies, comics, TV shows, toys – you name it. As an only child, Clyde envies Lincoln – how cool would it be to always have siblings around to talk to? But since Clyde spends so much time at the Loud household, he's almost an honorary sibling anyway. He also has a major crush on Lori.

HAROLD AND HOWARD McBRIDE
Clyde's Loving Dads

Harold and Howard are Clyde's loving dads and only want the best for him, but what they define as the best may differ. Harold is a level-headed straight-shooter with a heart of gold. The more easygoing of Clyde's dads, Harold often has to convince Howard that it's okay for them to not constantly hover over him. Howard is a constantly anxious helicopter parent and easy to break down into emotional sobbing, whether it be sad times (like when Clyde stubbed his toe) or happy (like when Clyde and Lincoln beat that really tough video game boss).Despite their differing parenting styles, the two dads bring nothing but love to the table.

CLEOPAWTRA
Clyde's Cat

NEPURRTITI
Clyde's Other Cat

SAM SHARP

Sam, 15, is Luna's classmate and good friend, who Luna has a crush on. Sam is all about the music – she loves to play guitar and write and compose music. Her favorite genre is rock and roll but she appreciates all good tunes. Unlike Luna, Sam only has one brother, Simon, but she thinks even one sibling provides enough chaos for her.

"PRIVATE EYES"

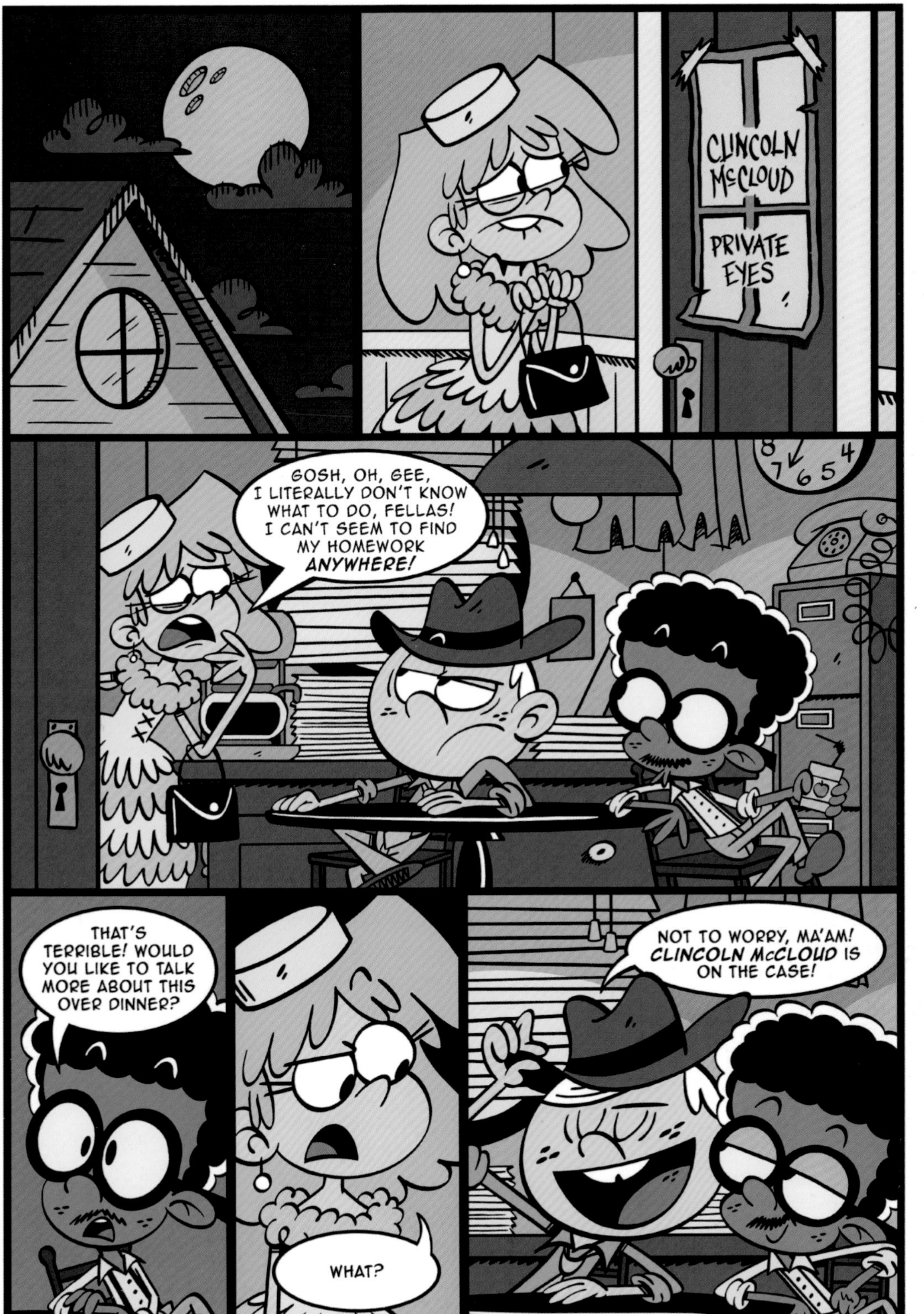
CLINCOLN McCLOUD
PRIVATE EYES
GOSH, OH, GEE, I LITERALLY DON'T KNOW WHAT TO DO, FELLAS! I CAN'T SEEM TO FIND MY HOMEWORK *ANYWHERE!*
THAT'S TERRIBLE! WOULD YOU LIKE TO TALK MORE ABOUT THIS OVER DINNER?
WHAT?
NOT TO WORRY, MA'AM! *CLINCOLN McCLOUD* IS ON THE CASE!

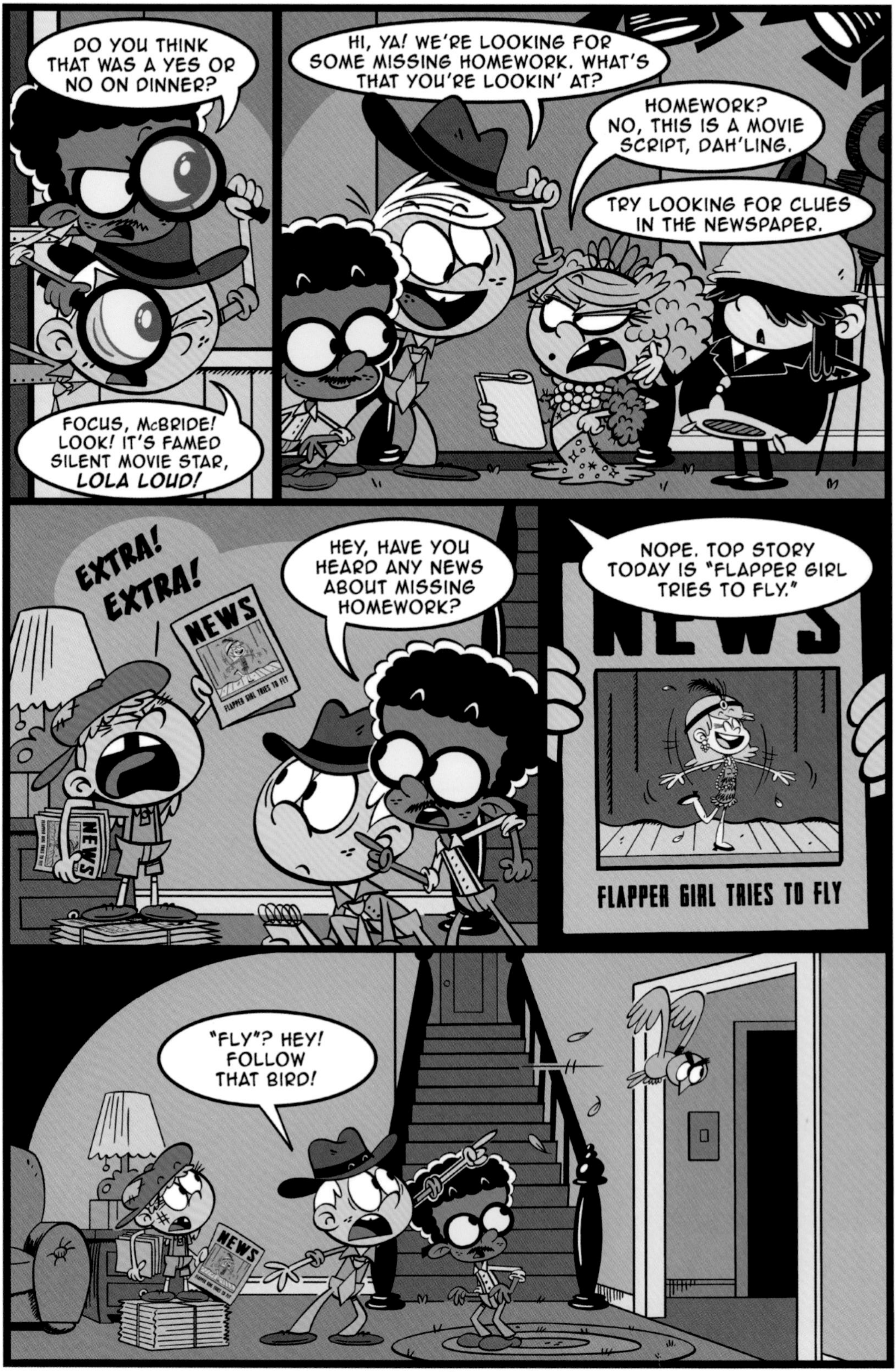
DO YOU THINK THAT WAS A YES OR NO ON DINNER?
FOCUS, McBRIDE! LOOK! IT'S FAMED SILENT MOVIE STAR, LOLA LOUD!
HI, YA! WE'RE LOOKING FOR SOME MISSING HOMEWORK. WHAT'S THAT YOU'RE LOOKIN' AT?
HOMEWORK? NO, THIS IS A MOVIE SCRIPT, DAH'LING.
TRY LOOKING FOR CLUES IN THE NEWSPAPER.
EXTRA! EXTRA!
NEWS
HEY, HAVE YOU HEARD ANY NEWS ABOUT MISSING HOMEWORK?
NOPE. TOP STORY TODAY IS "FLAPPER GIRL TRIES TO FLY."
NEWS
FLAPPER GIRL TRIES TO FLY
"FLY"? HEY! FOLLOW THAT BIRD!
NEWS

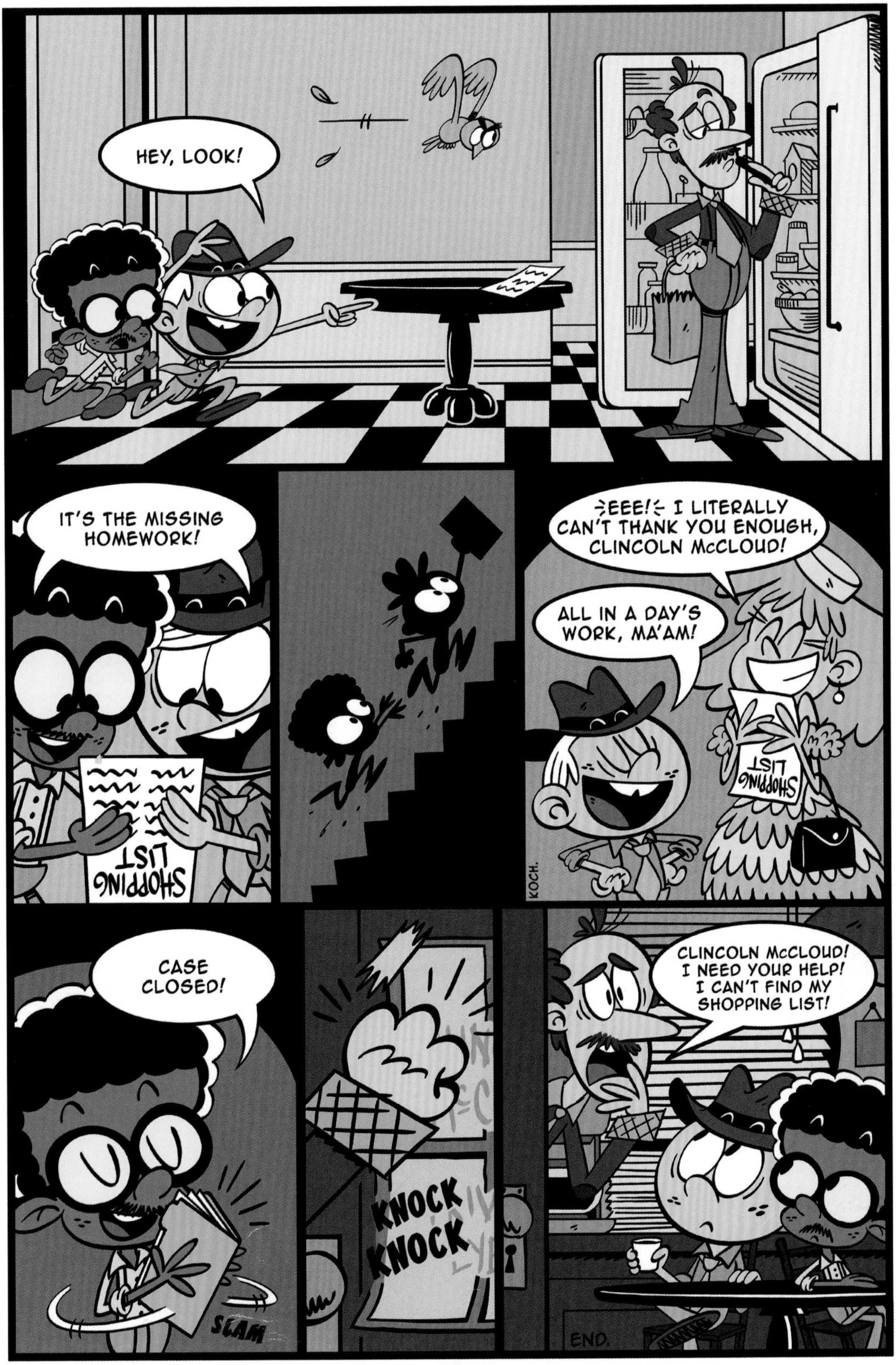
HEY, LOOK!
IT'S THE MISSING HOMEWORK!
SHOPPING LIST
EEE! I LITERALLY CAN'T THANK YOU ENOUGH, CLINCOLN McCLOUD!
ALL IN A DAY'S WORK, MA'AM!
SHOPPING LIST
KOCH.
CASE CLOSED!
SLAM
KNOCK KNOCK
CLINCOLN McCLOUD! I NEED YOUR HELP! I CAN'T FIND MY SHOPPING LIST!
END.

"MY YARD, MY PROPERTY"

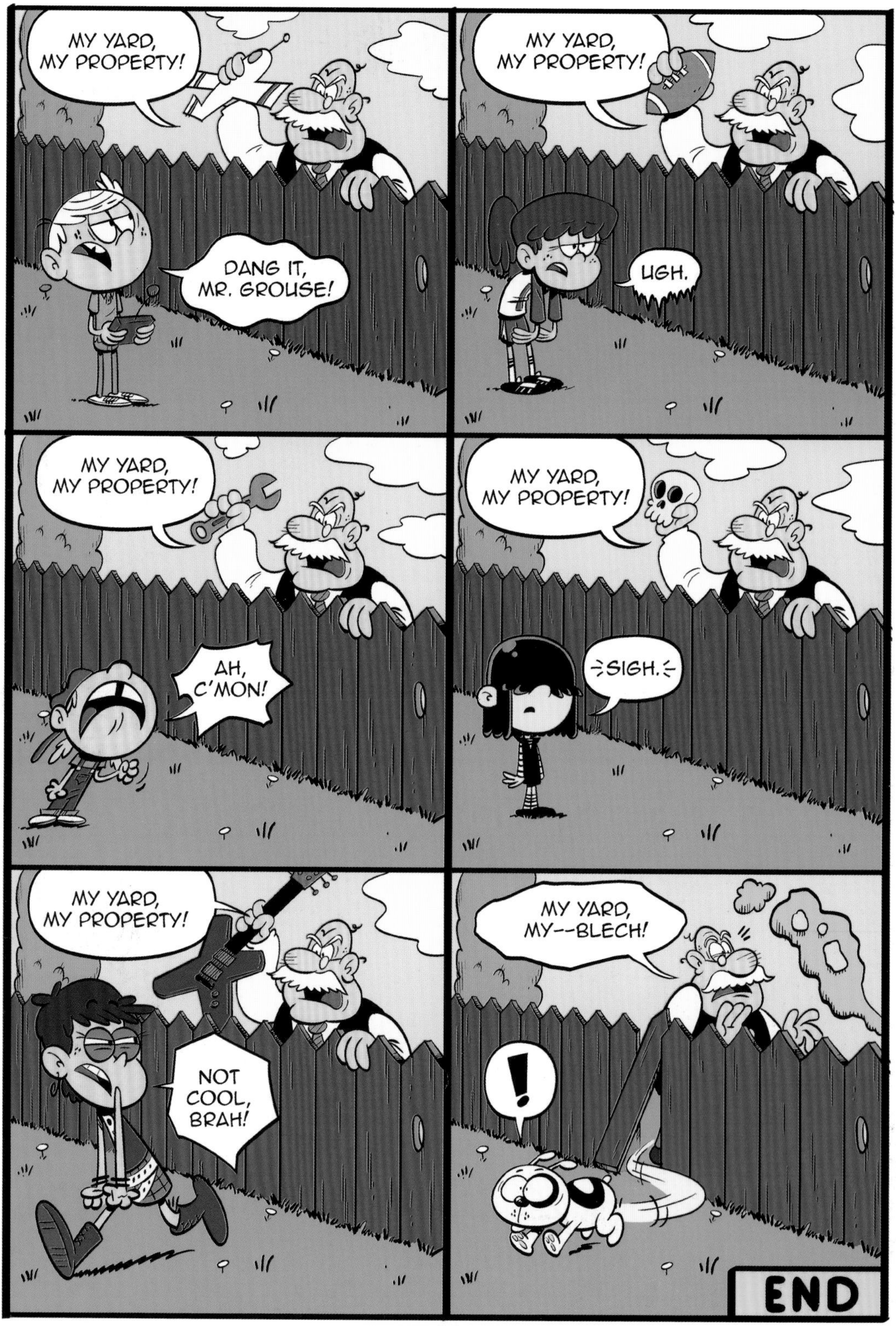
MY YARD, MY PROPERTY!
DANG IT, MR. GROUSE!
MY YARD, MY PROPERTY!
UGH.
MY YARD, MY PROPERTY!
AH, C'MON!
MY YARD, MY PROPERTY!
SIGH.
MY YARD, MY PROPERTY!
NOT COOL, BRAH!
MY YARD, MY--BLECH!
!
END

"A PIRATE'S LIFE FOR CJ"

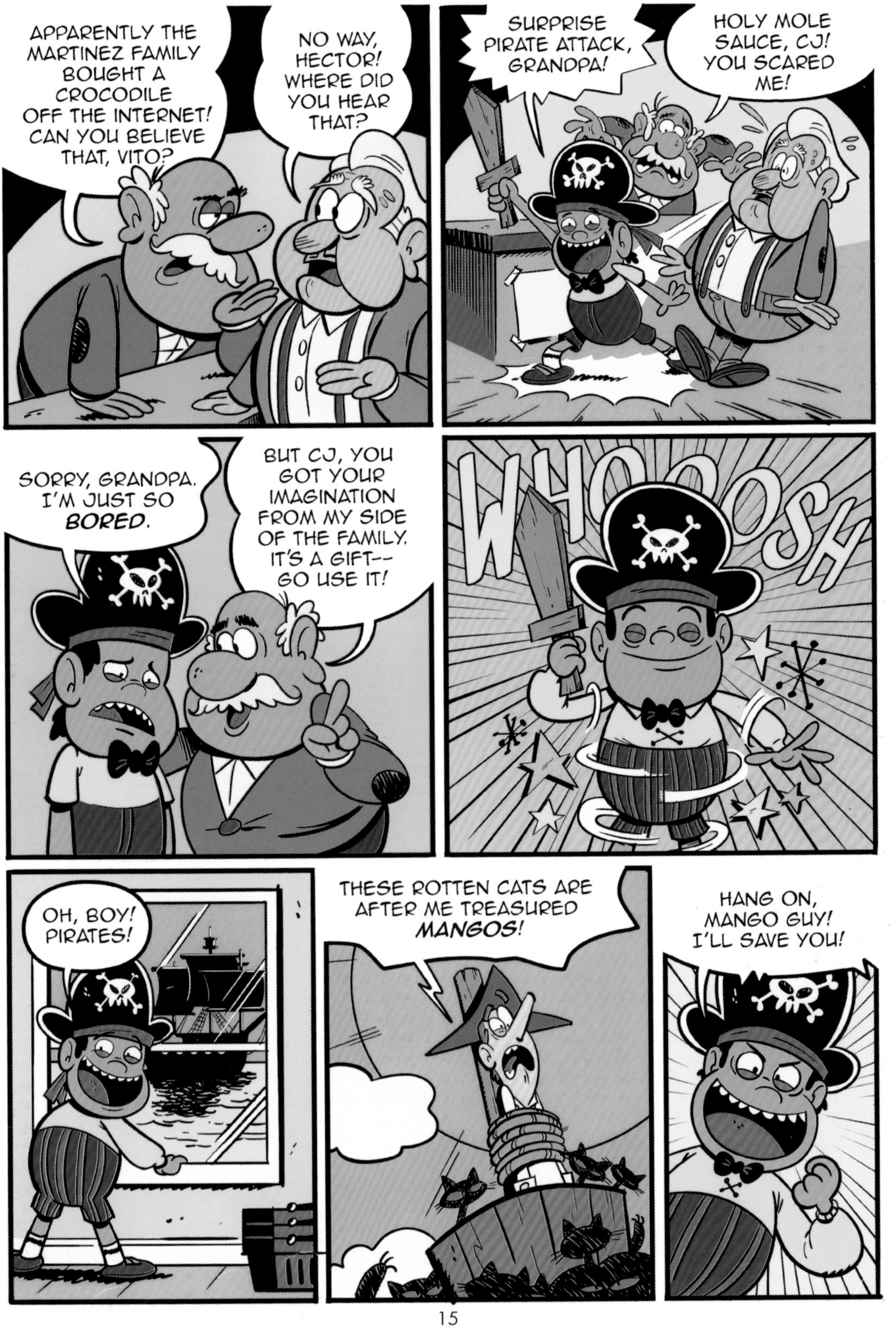
APPARENTLY THE MARTINEZ FAMILY BOUGHT A CROCODILE OFF THE INTERNET! CAN YOU BELIEVE THAT, VITO?
NO WAY, HECTOR! WHERE DID YOU HEAR THAT?
SURPRISE PIRATE ATTACK, GRANDPA!
HOLY MOLE SAUCE, CJ! YOU SCARED ME!
SORRY, GRANDPA. I'M JUST SO *BORED*.
BUT CJ, YOU GOT YOUR IMAGINATION FROM MY SIDE OF THE FAMILY. IT'S A GIFT-- GO USE IT!
WHOOOOSH
OH, BOY! PIRATES!
THESE ROTTEN CATS ARE AFTER ME TREASURED *MANGOS*!
HANG ON, MANGO GUY! I'LL SAVE YOU!

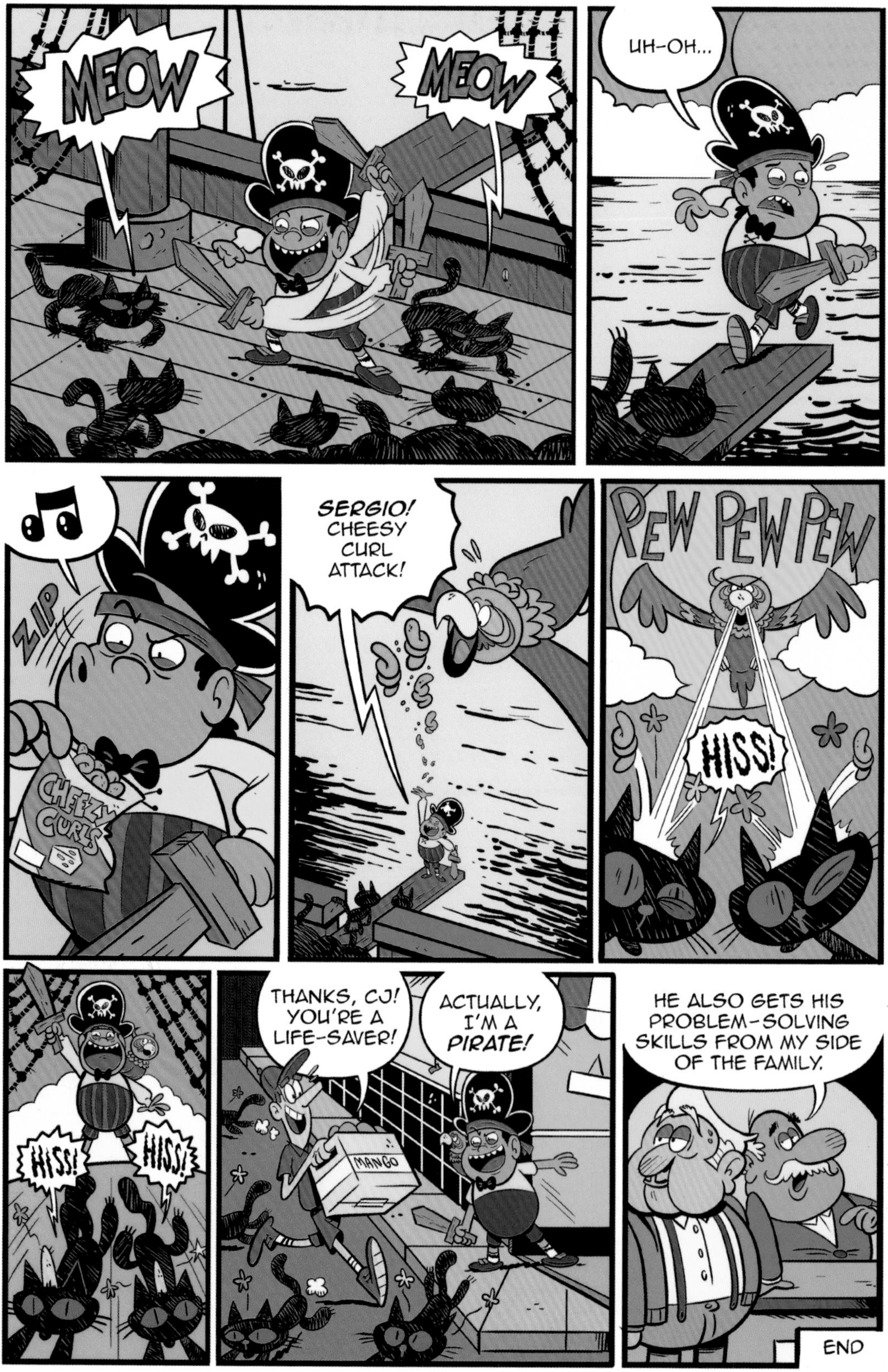
MEOW
MEOW
UH-OH...
ZIP
CHEEZY CURLS
SERGIO! CHEESY CURL ATTACK!
PEW PEW PEW
HISS!
HISS!
HISS!
THANKS, CJ! YOU'RE A LIFE-SAVER!
ACTUALLY, I'M A PIRATE!
MANGO
HE ALSO GETS HIS PROBLEM-SOLVING SKILLS FROM MY SIDE OF THE FAMILY.
END

"HICCUP HIJINKS"

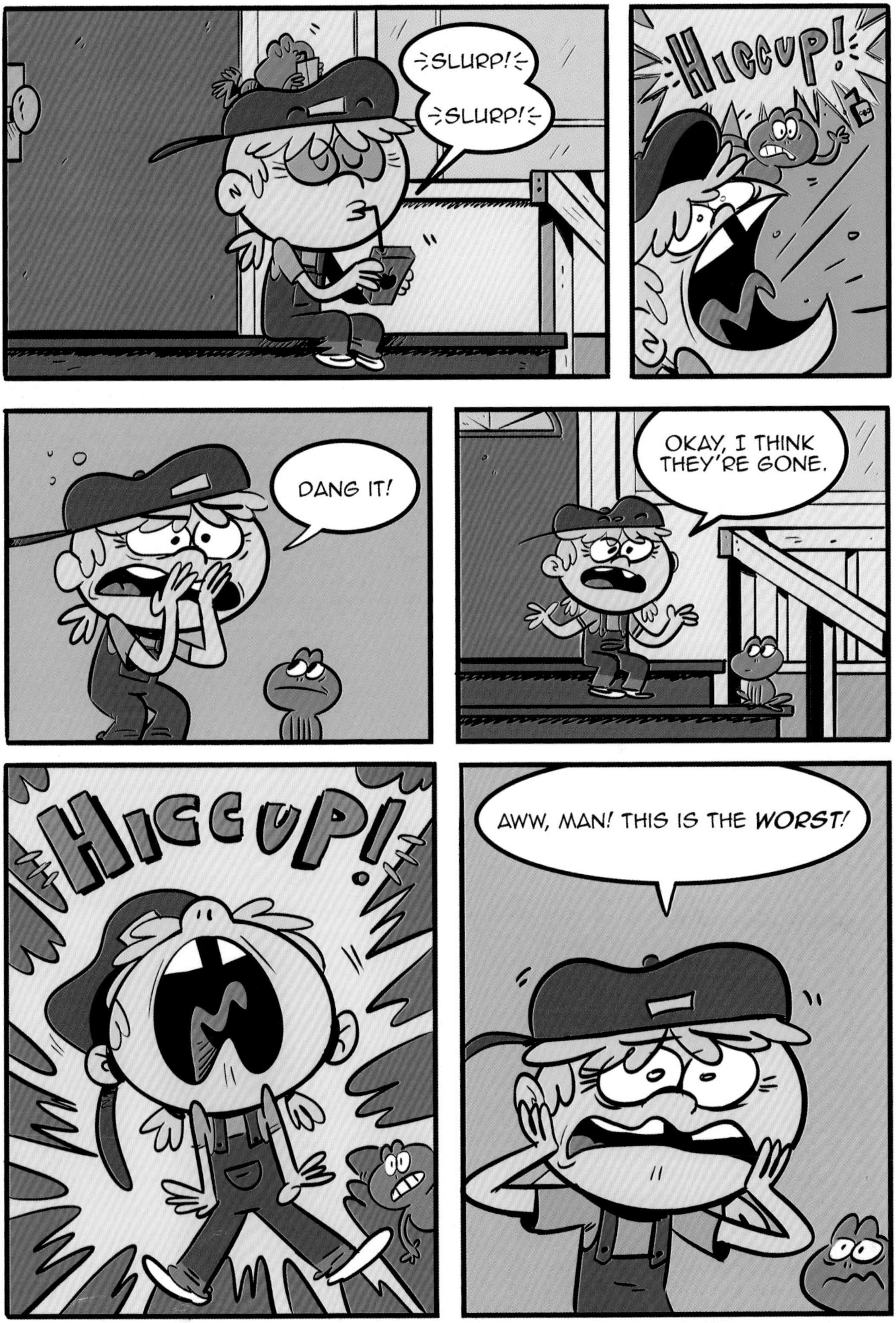
SLURP!
SLURP!
HICCUP!
DANG IT!
OKAY, I THINK THEY'RE GONE.
HICCUP!
AWW, MAN! THIS IS THE *WORST*!

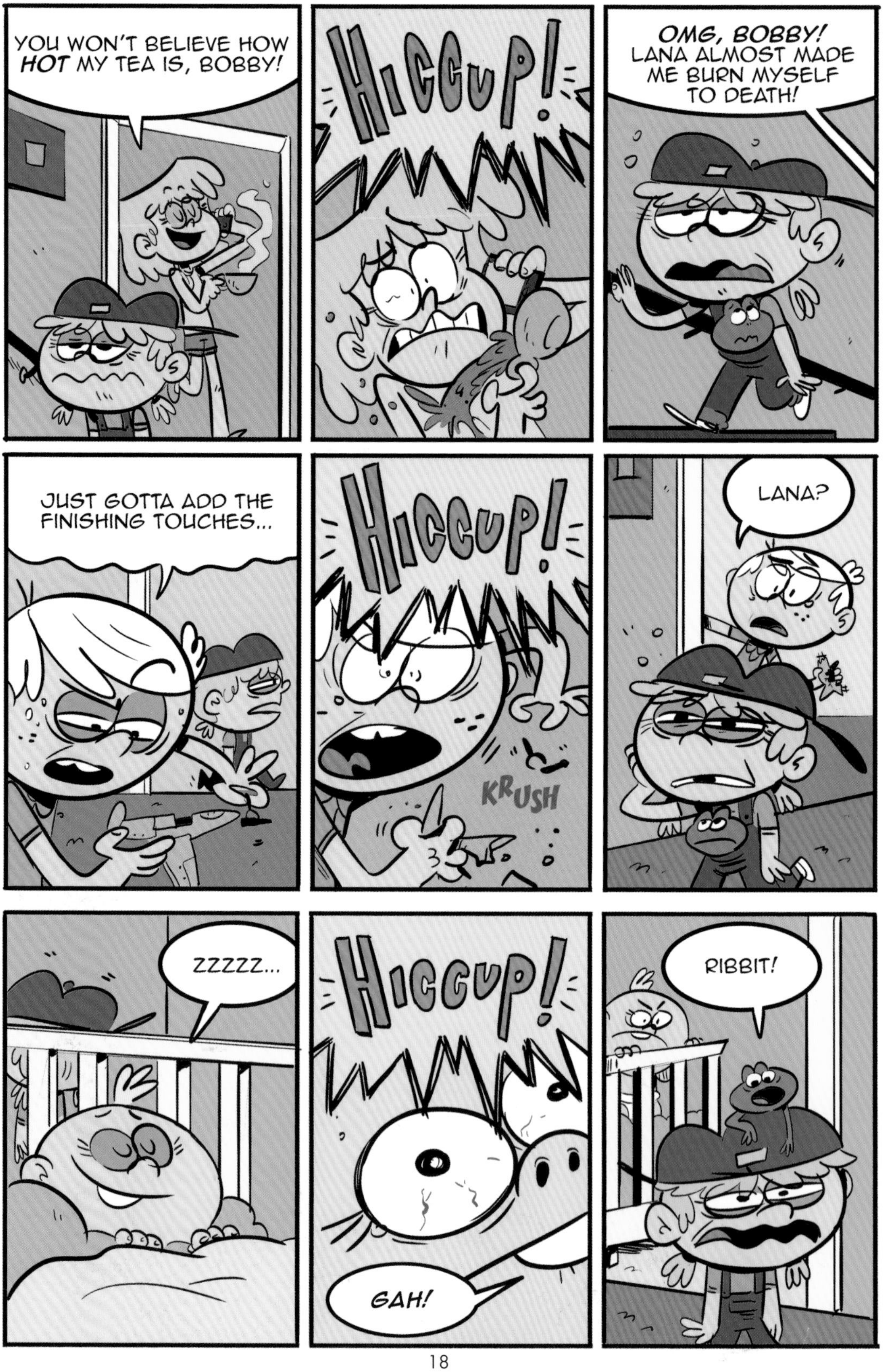
YOU WON'T BELIEVE HOW *HOT* MY TEA IS, BOBBY!
HICCUP!
OMG, BOBBY! LANA ALMOST MADE ME BURN MYSELF TO DEATH!
JUST GOTTA ADD THE FINISHING TOUCHES...
HICCUP!
KRUSH
LANA?
ZZZZZ...
HICCUP!
GAH!
RIBBIT!

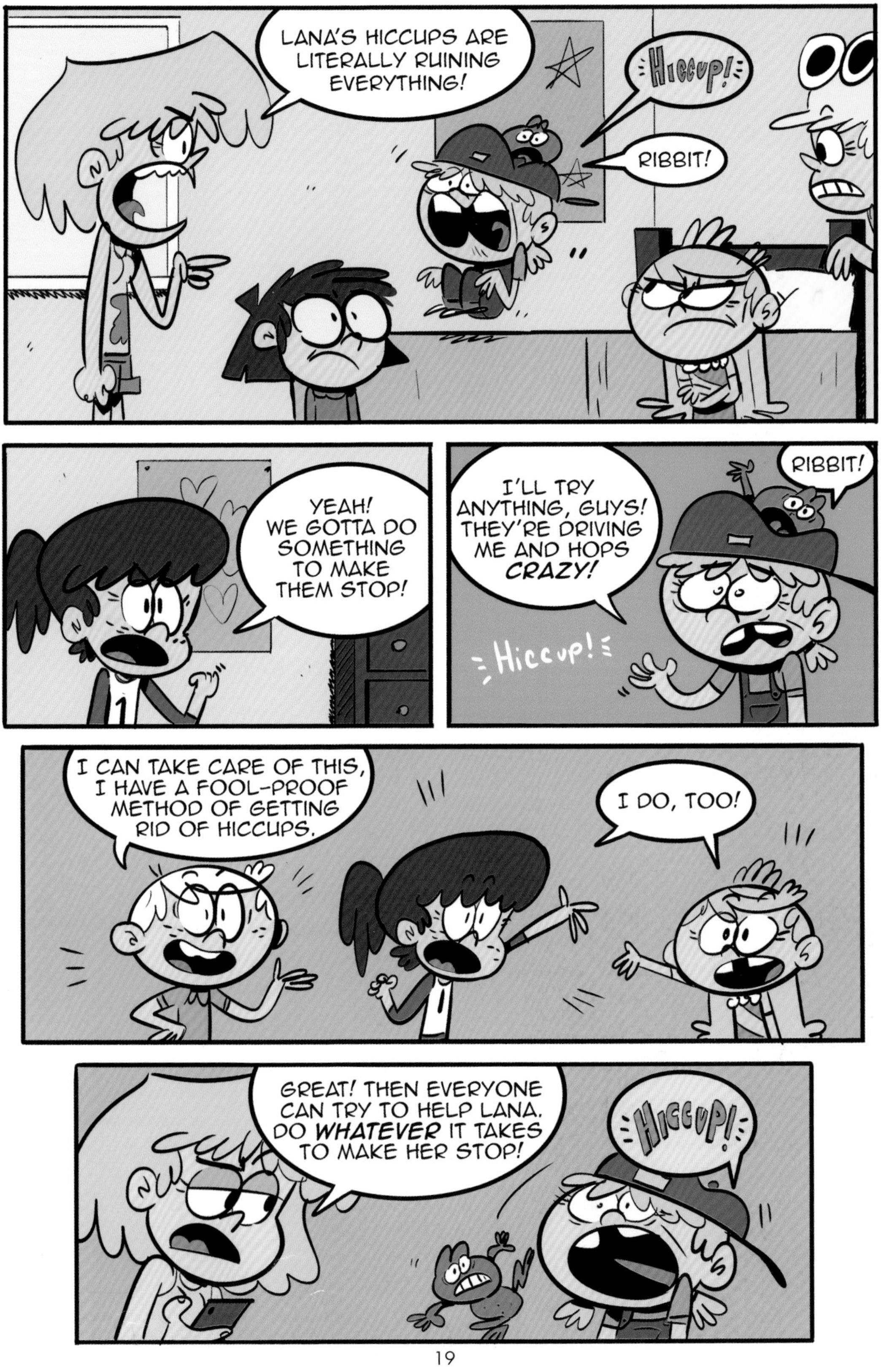
LANA'S HICCUPS ARE LITERALLY RUINING EVERYTHING!
HICCUP!
RIBBIT!
YEAH! WE GOTTA DO SOMETHING TO MAKE THEM STOP!
I'LL TRY ANYTHING, GUYS! THEY'RE DRIVING ME AND HOPS *CRAZY!*
RIBBIT!
HICCUP!
I CAN TAKE CARE OF THIS, I HAVE A FOOL-PROOF METHOD OF GETTING RID OF HICCUPS.
I DO, TOO!
GREAT! THEN EVERYONE CAN TRY TO HELP LANA. DO *WHATEVER* IT TAKES TO MAKE HER STOP!
HICCUP!

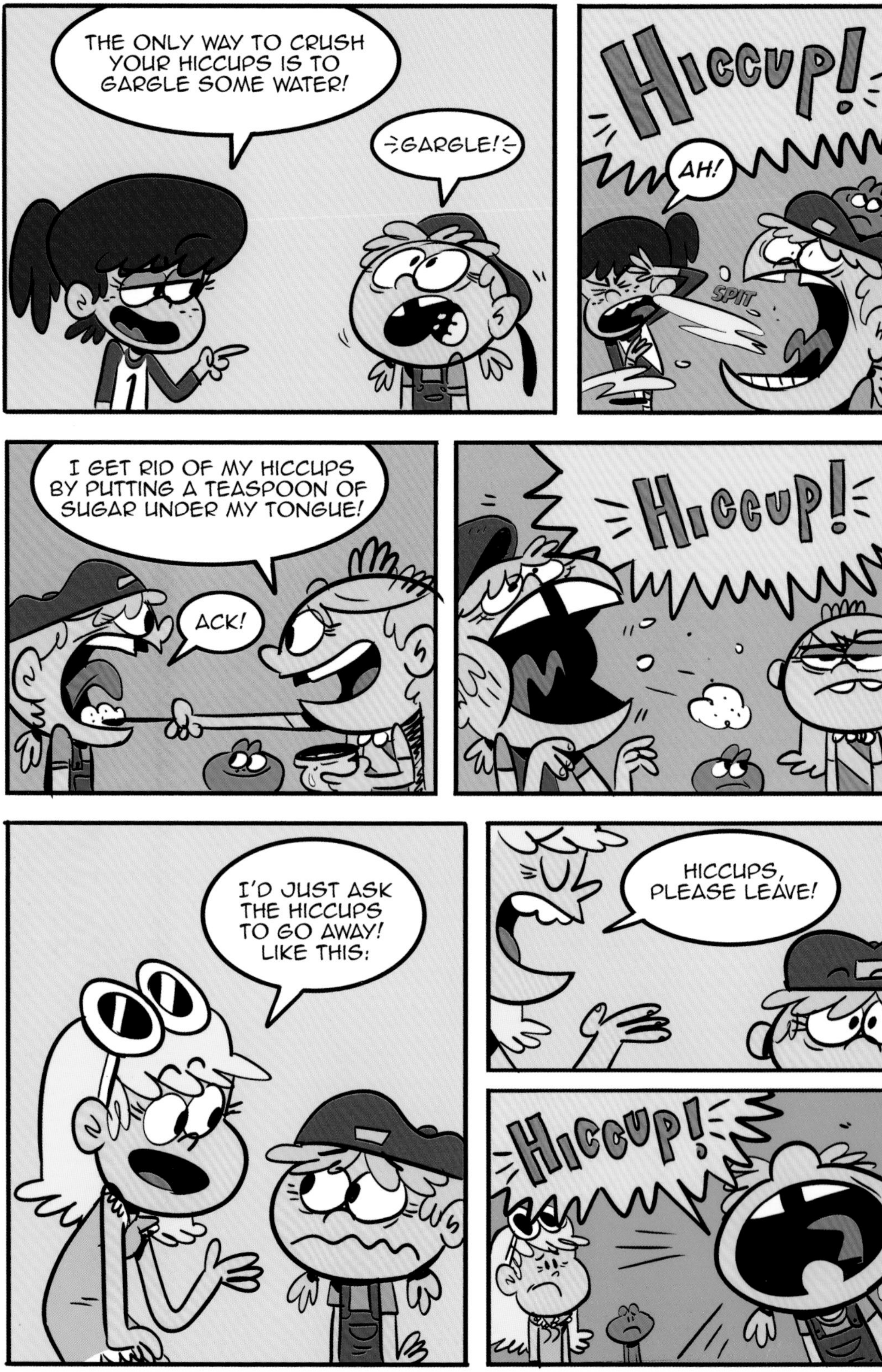
THE ONLY WAY TO CRUSH YOUR HICCUPS IS TO GARGLE SOME WATER!
GARGLE!
HICCUP!
AH!
SPIT
I GET RID OF MY HICCUPS BY PUTTING A TEASPOON OF SUGAR UNDER MY TONGUE!
ACK!
HICCUP!
I'D JUST ASK THE HICCUPS TO GO AWAY! LIKE THIS:
HICCUPS, PLEASE LEAVE!
HICCUP!

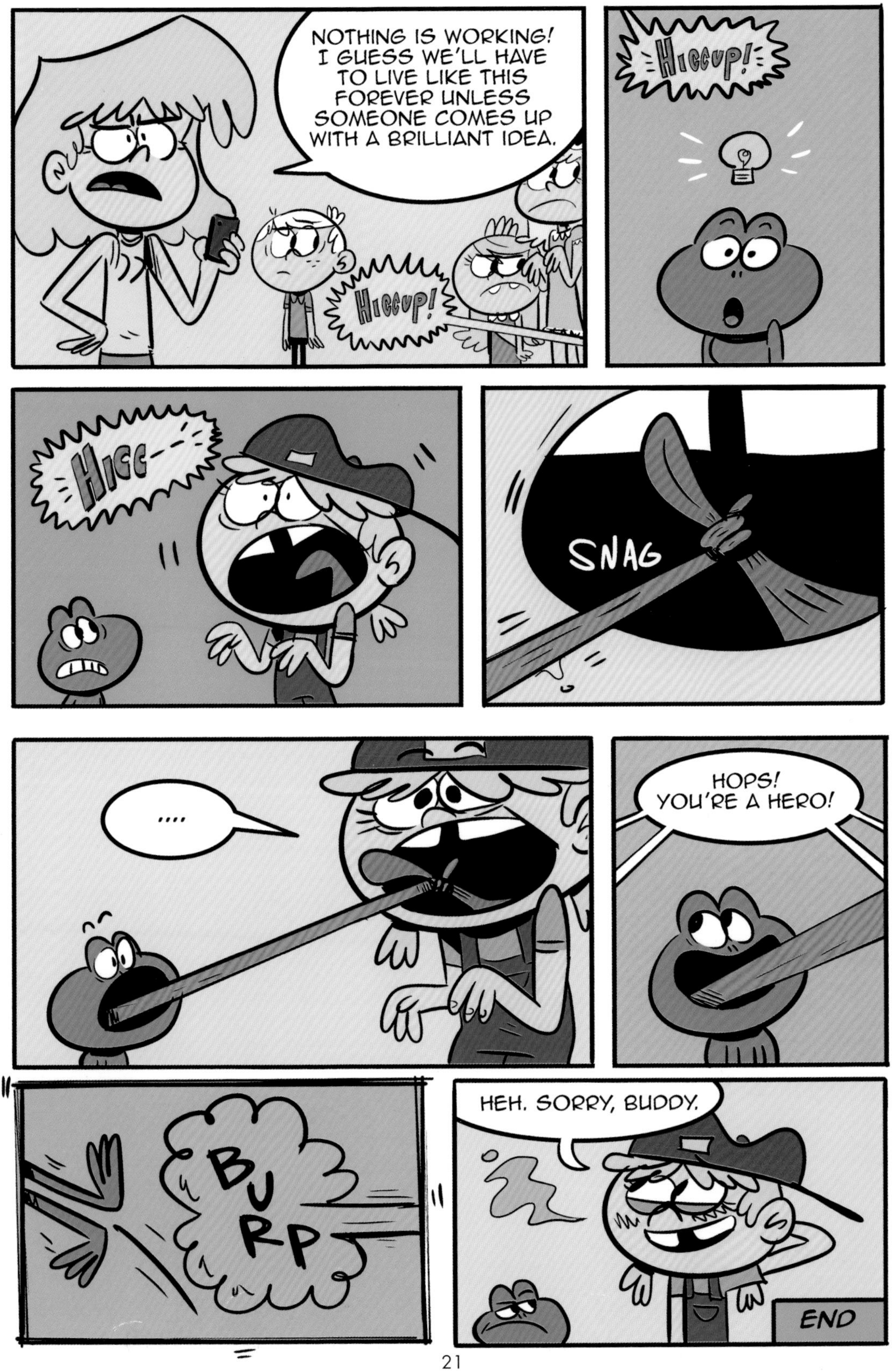
NOTHING IS WORKING! I GUESS WE'LL HAVE TO LIVE LIKE THIS FOREVER UNLESS SOMEONE COMES UP WITH A BRILLIANT IDEA.
HICCUP!
HICCUP!
HICC--
SNAG
....
HOPS! YOU'RE A HERO!
BURP
HEH. SORRY, BUDDY.
END

"MOM'S NIGHT IN"

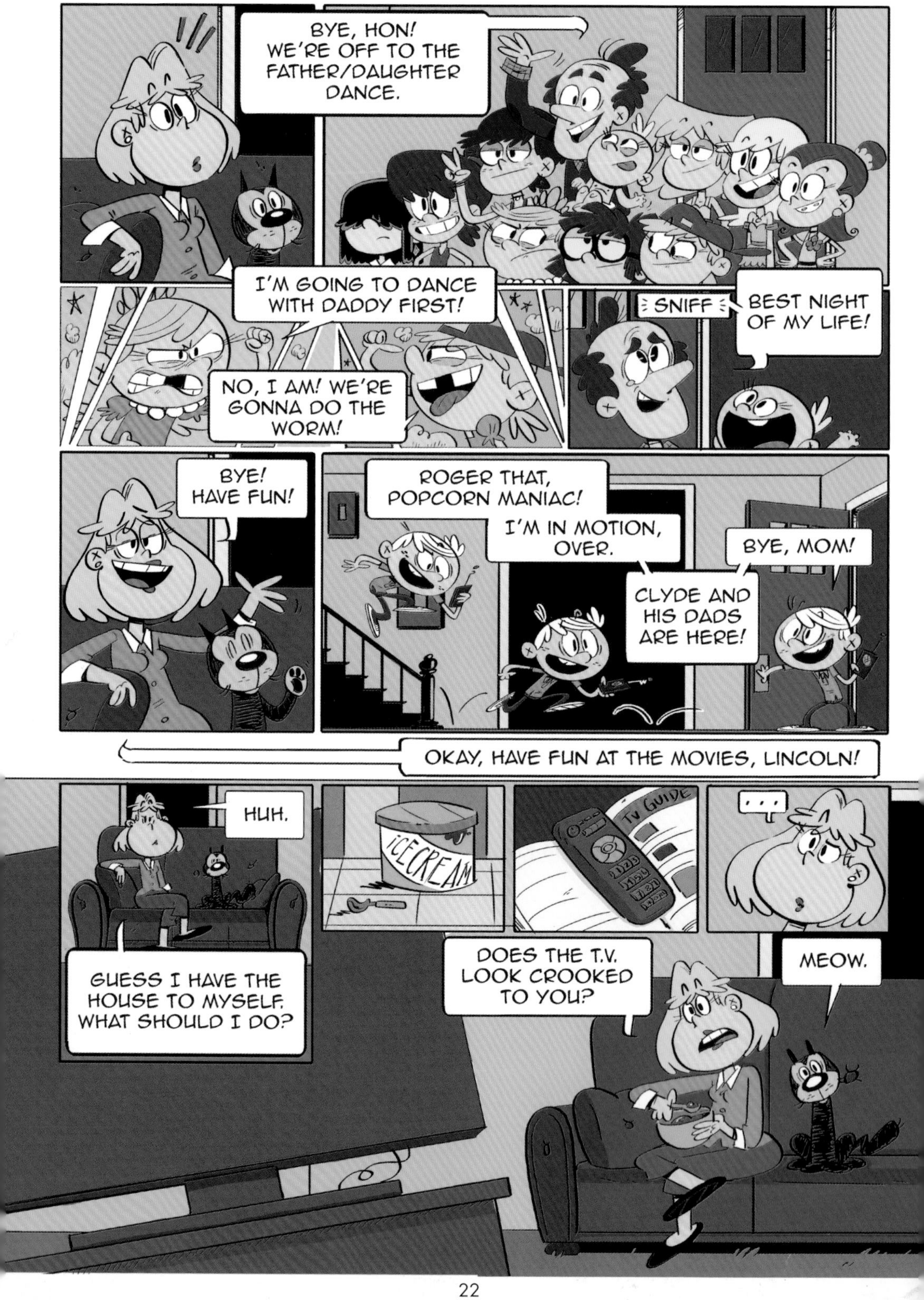

BYE, HON! WE'RE OFF TO THE FATHER/DAUGHTER DANCE.
I'M GOING TO DANCE WITH DADDY FIRST!
NO, I AM! WE'RE GONNA DO THE WORM!
SNIFF
BEST NIGHT OF MY LIFE!
BYE! HAVE FUN!
ROGER THAT, POPCORN MANIAC!
I'M IN MOTION, OVER.
CLYDE AND HIS DADS ARE HERE!
BYE, MOM!
OKAY, HAVE FUN AT THE MOVIES, LINCOLN!
HUH.
GUESS I HAVE THE HOUSE TO MYSELF. WHAT SHOULD I DO?
ICE CREAM
TV GUIDE
...
DOES THE T.V. LOOK CROOKED TO YOU?
MEOW.

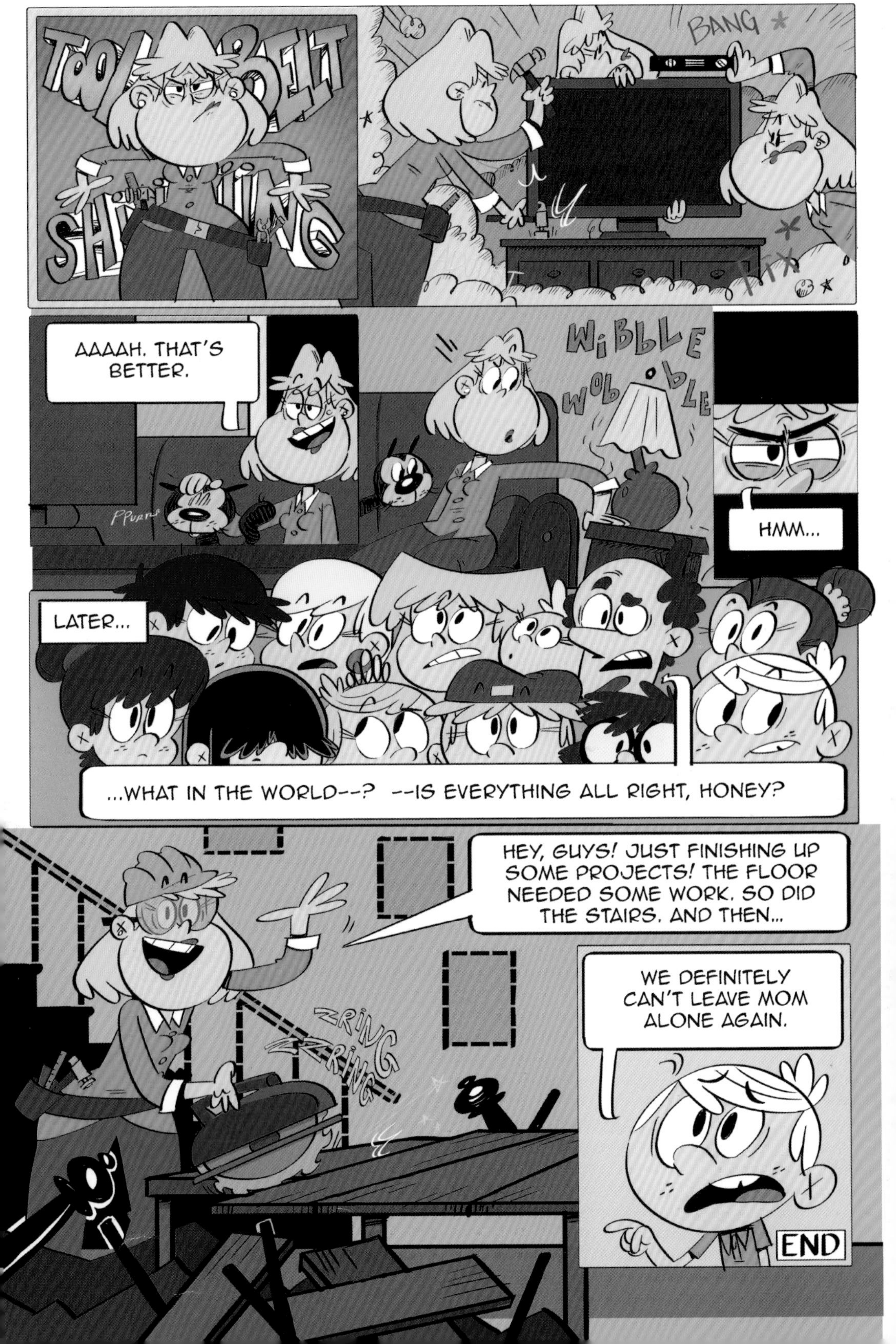
TOOL BELT
SHING
BANG
AAAAH. THAT'S BETTER.
WIBBLE WOBBLE
HMM...
LATER...
...WHAT IN THE WORLD--? --IS EVERYTHING ALL RIGHT, HONEY?
HEY, GUYS! JUST FINISHING UP SOME PROJECTS! THE FLOOR NEEDED SOME WORK. SO DID THE STAIRS. AND THEN...
ZRING ZRING
WE DEFINITELY CAN'T LEAVE MOM ALONE AGAIN.
END

"GOTH PERKS"

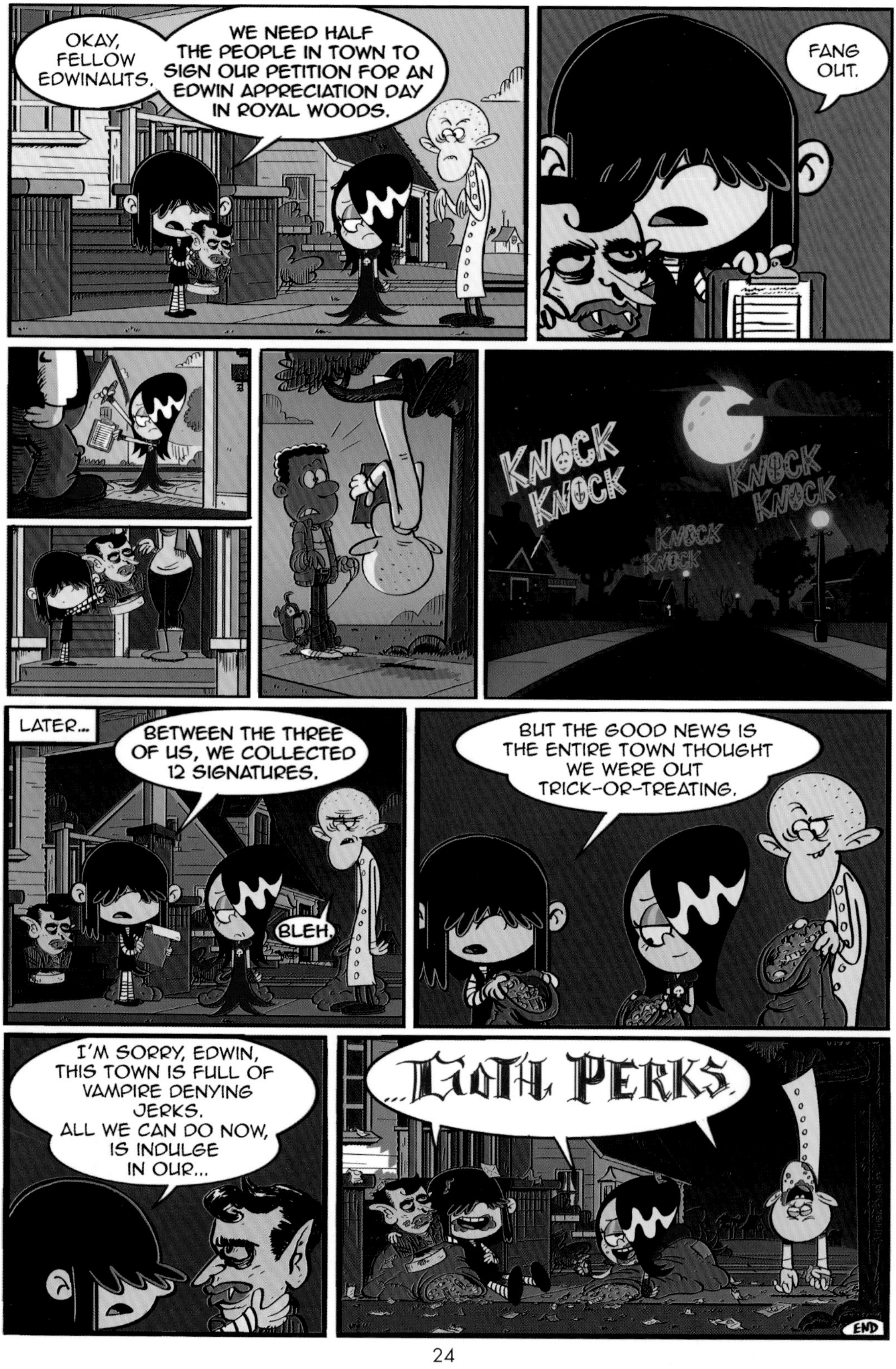

OKAY, FELLOW EDWINAUTS.
WE NEED HALF THE PEOPLE IN TOWN TO SIGN OUR PETITION FOR AN EDWIN APPRECIATION DAY IN ROYAL WOODS.
FANG OUT.
KNOCK KNOCK
KNOCK KNOCK
KNOCK KNOCK
LATER...
BETWEEN THE THREE OF US, WE COLLECTED 12 SIGNATURES.
BLEH.
BUT THE GOOD NEWS IS THE ENTIRE TOWN THOUGHT WE WERE OUT TRICK-OR-TREATING.
I'M SORRY, EDWIN, THIS TOWN IS FULL OF VAMPIRE DENYING JERKS. ALL WE CAN DO NOW, IS INDULGE IN OUR...
...GOTH PERKS.
END

"BABY BROTHER"

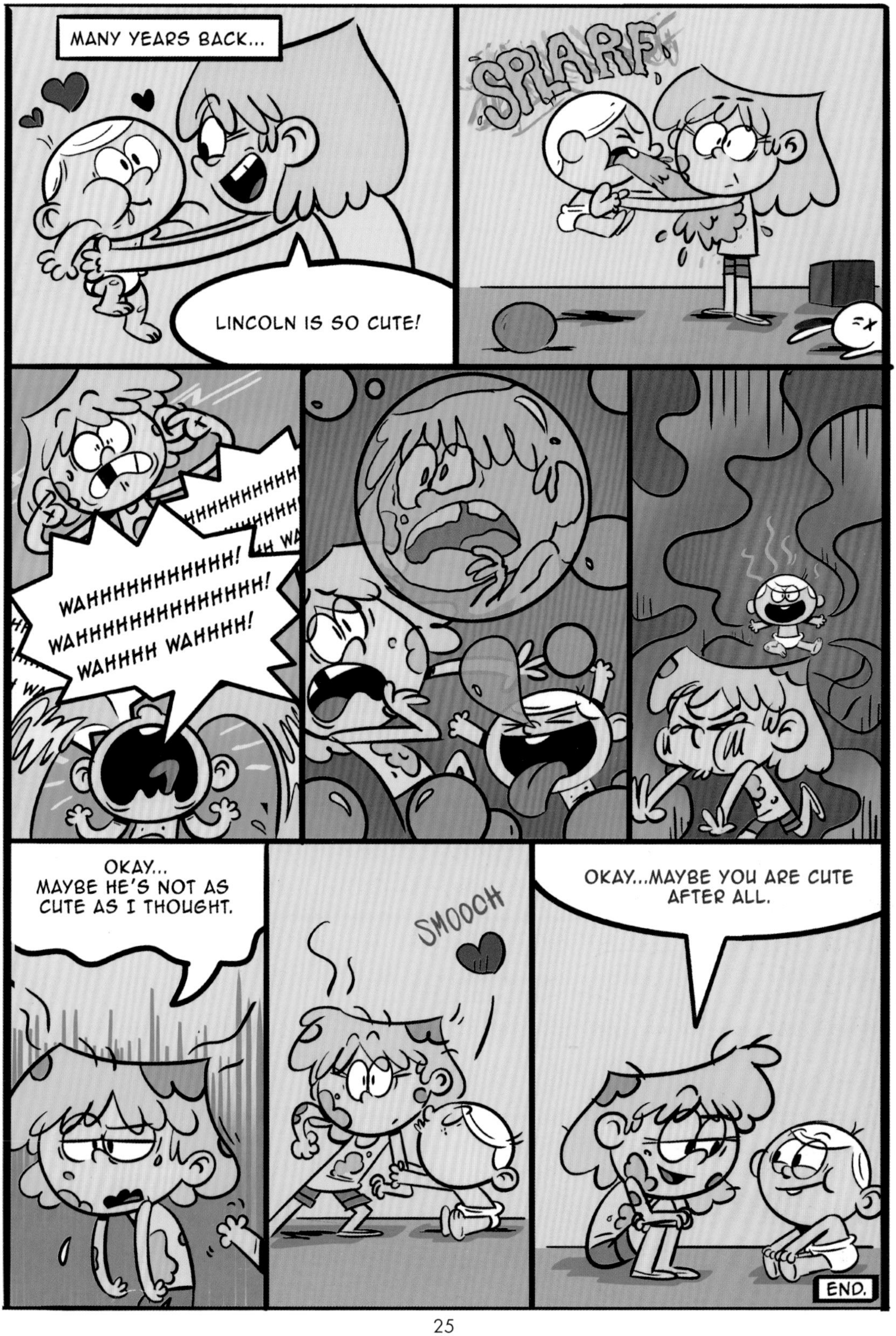

MANY YEARS BACK...
LINCOLN IS SO CUTE!
SPLARF
WAHHHHHHHHHHHH! WAHHHHHHHHHHHHHH! WAHHHHH WAHHHH!
OKAY... MAYBE HE'S NOT AS CUTE AS I THOUGHT.
SMOOCH
OKAY...MAYBE YOU ARE CUTE AFTER ALL.
END.

"CLOWNING AROUND"

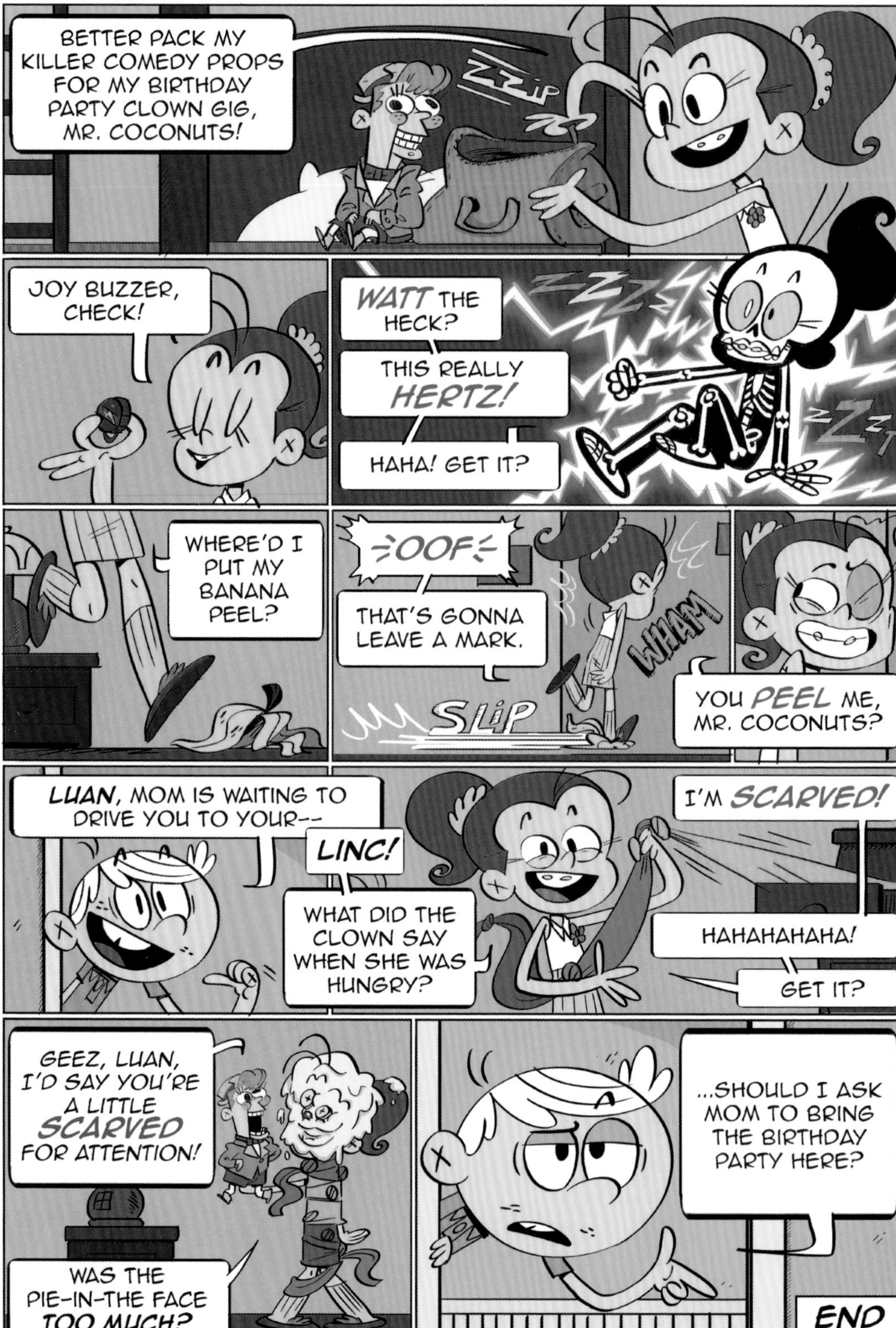
BETTER PACK MY KILLER COMEDY PROPS FOR MY BIRTHDAY PARTY CLOWN GIG, MR. COCONUTS!
ZZIP
JOY BUZZER, CHECK!
WATT THE HECK?
THIS REALLY HERTZ!
HAHA! GET IT?
ZZZZ
ZZZT
WHERE'D I PUT MY BANANA PEEL?
OOF
THAT'S GONNA LEAVE A MARK.
SLIP
WHAM
YOU PEEL ME, MR. COCONUTS?
LUAN, MOM IS WAITING TO DRIVE YOU TO YOUR--
LINC!
WHAT DID THE CLOWN SAY WHEN SHE WAS HUNGRY?
I'M SCARVED!
HAHAHAHAHA!
GET IT?
GEEZ, LUAN, I'D SAY YOU'RE A LITTLE SCARVED FOR ATTENTION!
WAS THE PIE-IN-THE FACE TOO MUCH?
...SHOULD I ASK MOM TO BRING THE BIRTHDAY PARTY HERE?
END

"BABES IN THE CITY"

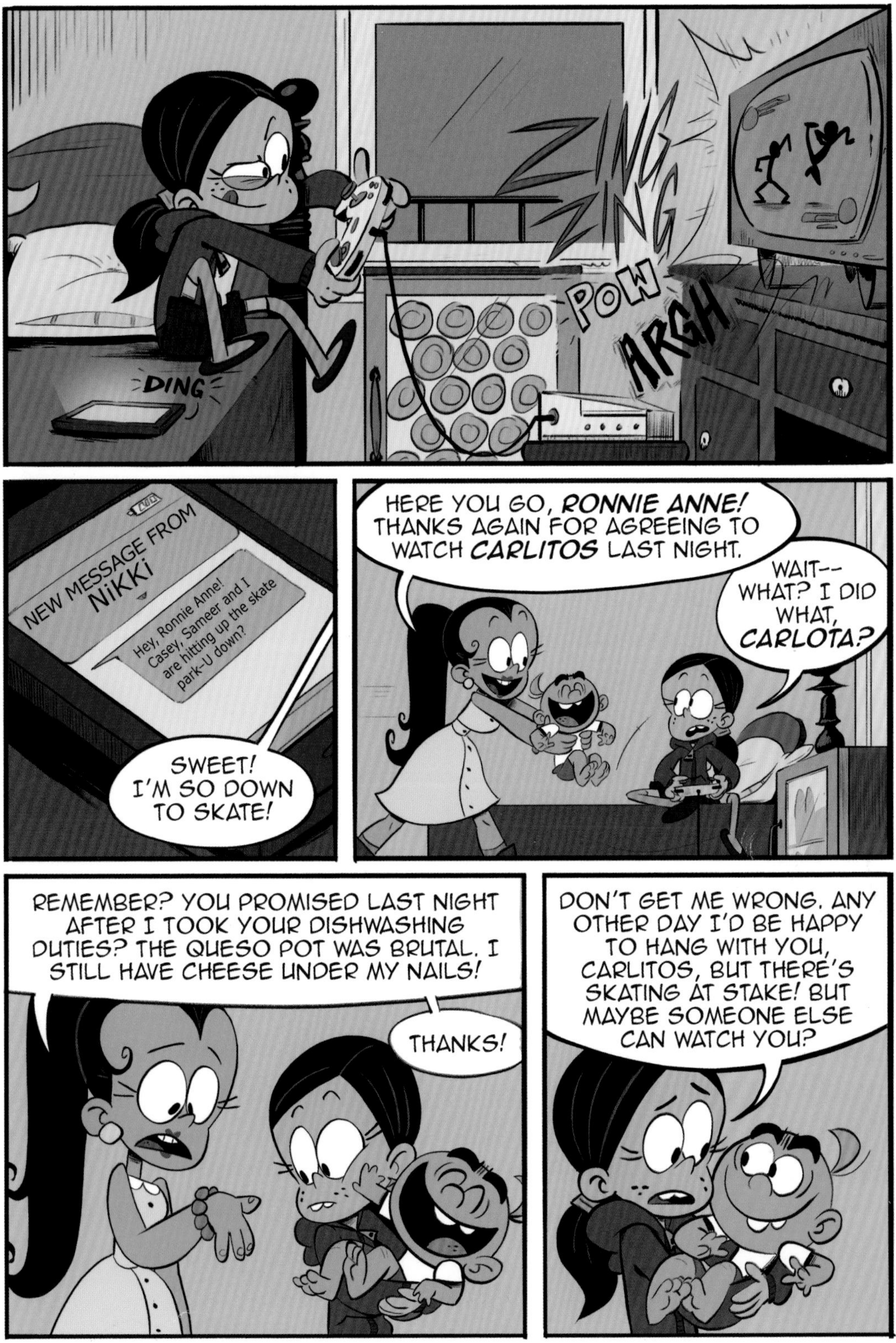

ZING
ZING
POW
ARGH
DING
NEW MESSAGE FROM
NiKKi
Hey, Ronnie Anne! Casey, Sameer and I are hitting up the skate park-U down?
SWEET! I'M SO DOWN TO SKATE!
HERE YOU GO, RONNIE ANNE! THANKS AGAIN FOR AGREEING TO WATCH CARLITOS LAST NIGHT.
WAIT-- WHAT? I DID WHAT, CARLOTA?
REMEMBER? YOU PROMISED LAST NIGHT AFTER I TOOK YOUR DISHWASHING DUTIES? THE QUESO POT WAS BRUTAL. I STILL HAVE CHEESE UNDER MY NAILS!
THANKS!
DON'T GET ME WRONG. ANY OTHER DAY I'D BE HAPPY TO HANG WITH YOU, CARLITOS, BUT THERE'S SKATING AT STAKE! BUT MAYBE SOMEONE ELSE CAN WATCH YOU?

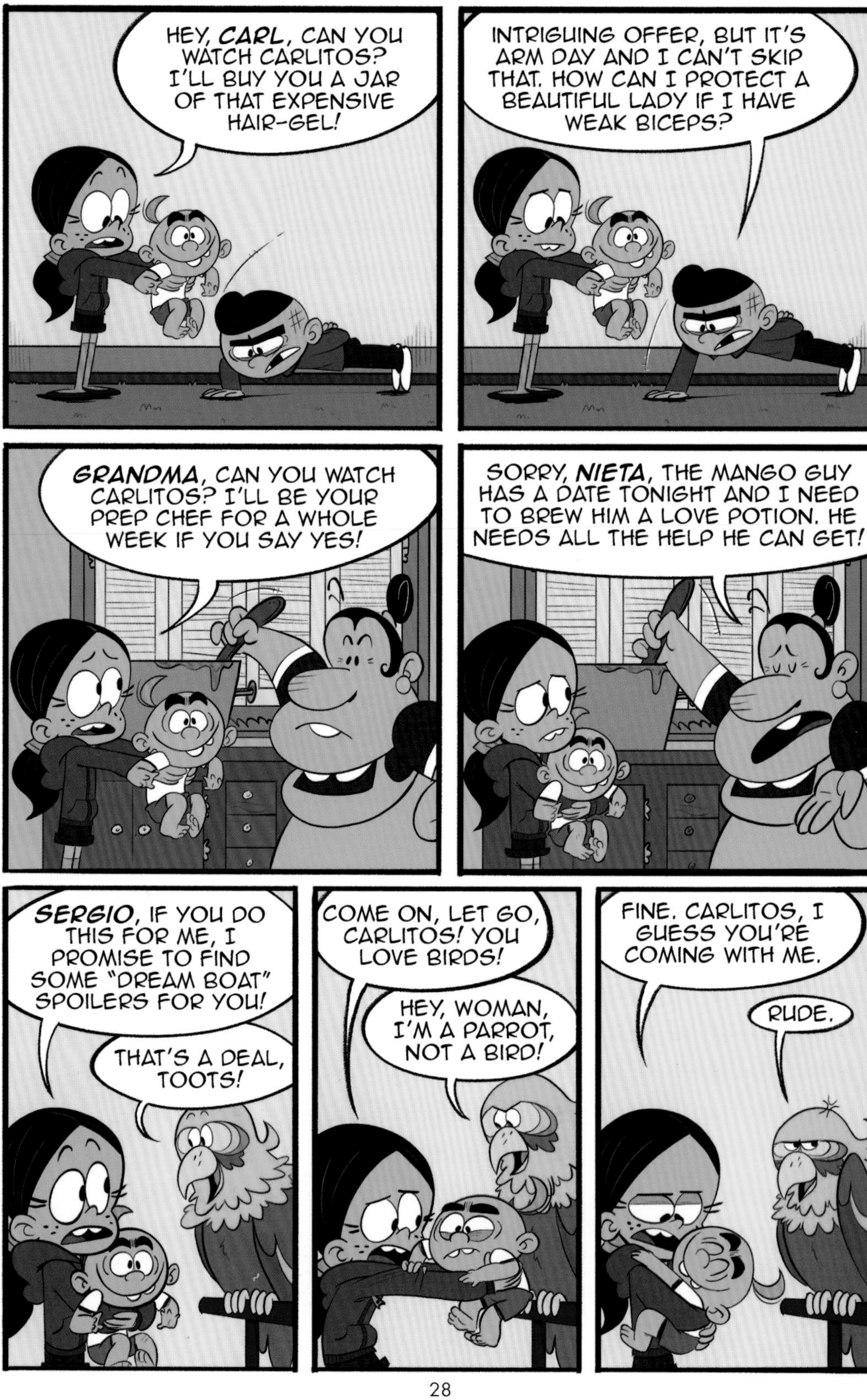
HEY, CARL, CAN YOU WATCH CARLITOS? I'LL BUY YOU A JAR OF THAT EXPENSIVE HAIR-GEL!
INTRIGUING OFFER, BUT IT'S ARM DAY AND I CAN'T SKIP THAT. HOW CAN I PROTECT A BEAUTIFUL LADY IF I HAVE WEAK BICEPS?
GRANDMA, CAN YOU WATCH CARLITOS? I'LL BE YOUR PREP CHEF FOR A WHOLE WEEK IF YOU SAY YES!
SORRY, NIETA, THE MANGO GUY HAS A DATE TONIGHT AND I NEED TO BREW HIM A LOVE POTION. HE NEEDS ALL THE HELP HE CAN GET!
SERGIO, IF YOU DO THIS FOR ME, I PROMISE TO FIND SOME "DREAM BOAT" SPOILERS FOR YOU!
THAT'S A DEAL, TOOTS!
COME ON, LET GO, CARLITOS! YOU LOVE BIRDS!
HEY, WOMAN, I'M A PARROT, NOT A BIRD!
FINE. CARLITOS, I GUESS YOU'RE COMING WITH ME.
RUDE.

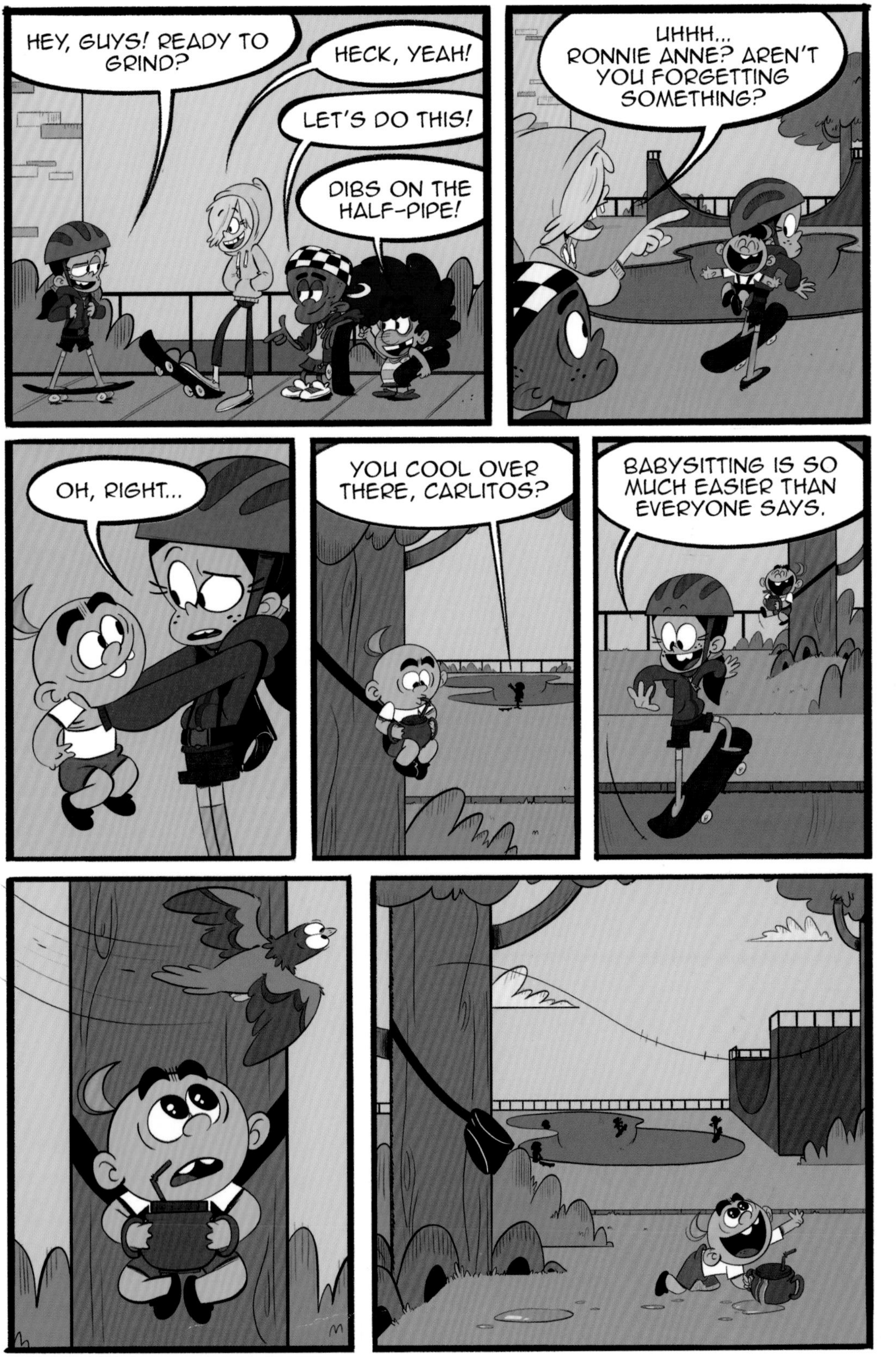
HEY, GUYS! READY TO GRIND?
HECK, YEAH!
LET'S DO THIS!
DIBS ON THE HALF-PIPE!
UHHH... RONNIE ANNE? AREN'T YOU FORGETTING SOMETHING?
OH, RIGHT...
YOU COOL OVER THERE, CARLITOS?
BABYSITTING IS SO MUCH EASIER THAN EVERYONE SAYS.

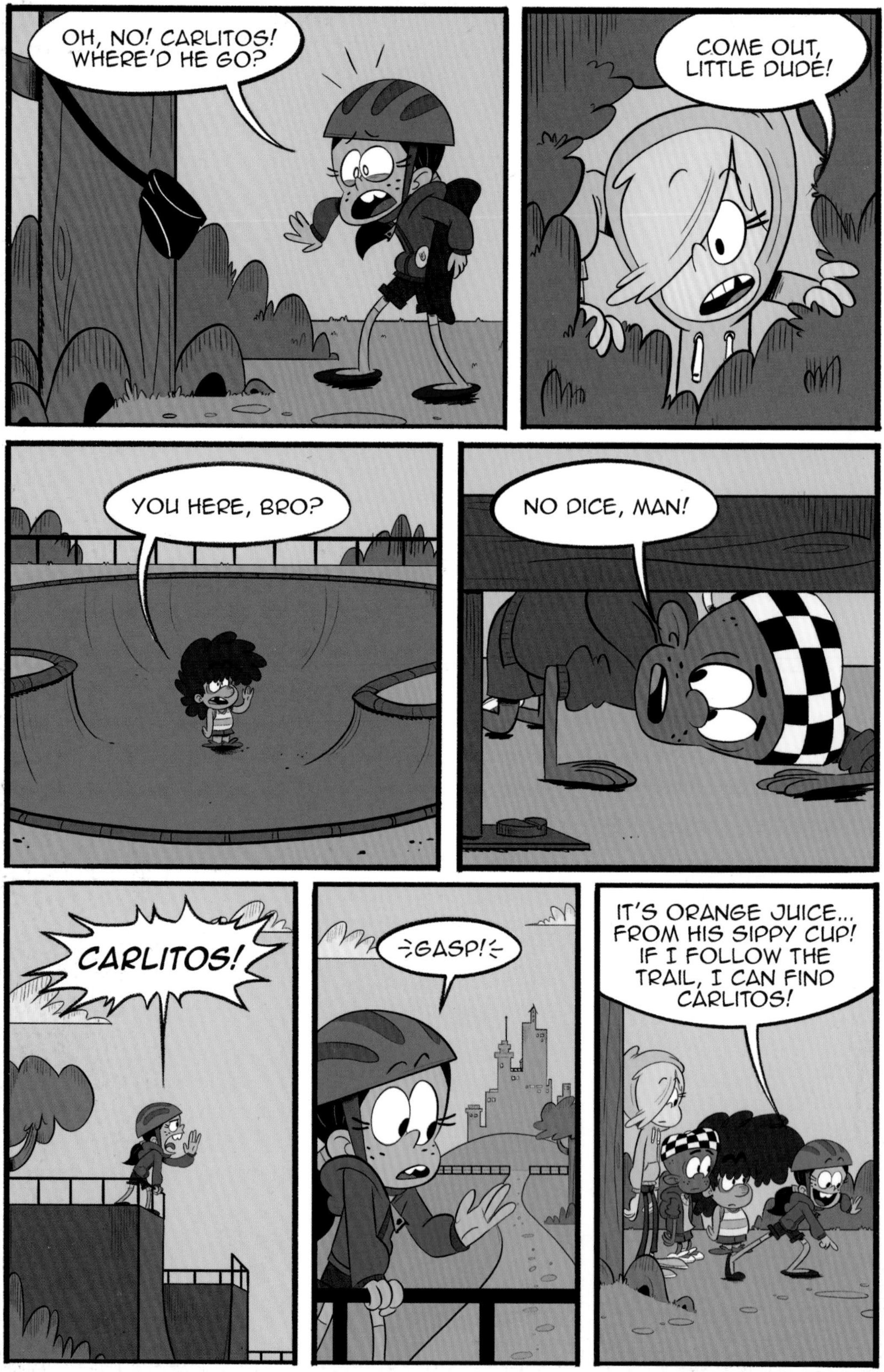
OH, NO! CARLITOS! WHERE'D HE GO?
COME OUT, LITTLE DUDE!
YOU HERE, BRO?
NO DICE, MAN!
CARLITOS!
GASP!
IT'S ORANGE JUICE... FROM HIS SIPPY CUP! IF I FOLLOW THE TRAIL, I CAN FIND CARLITOS!

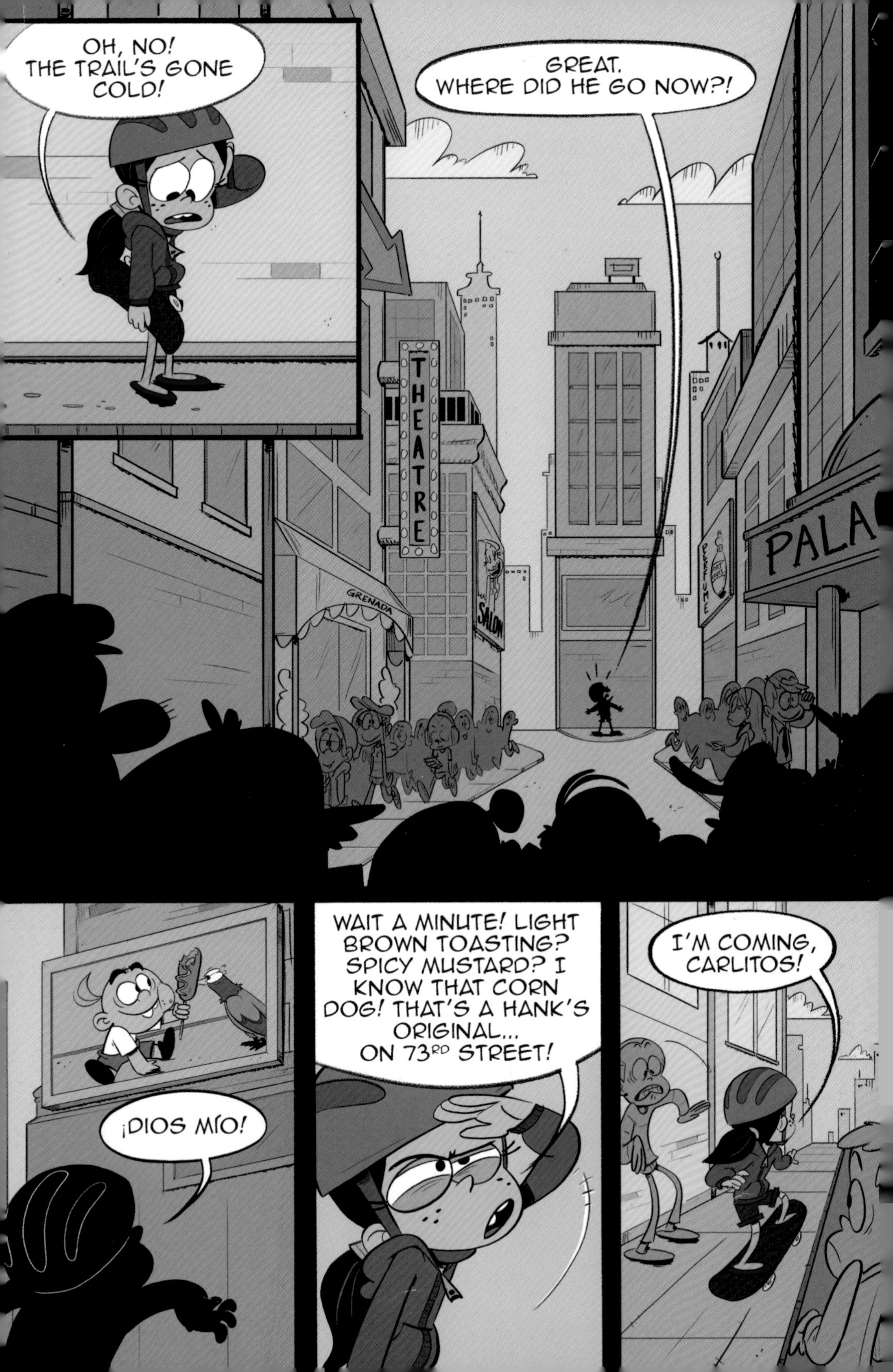
OH, NO! THE TRAIL'S GONE COLD!
GREAT. WHERE DID HE GO NOW?!
THEATRE
GRENADA
SALON
PERFUME
PALA
¡DIOS MÍO!
WAIT A MINUTE! LIGHT BROWN TOASTING? SPICY MUSTARD? I KNOW THAT CORN DOG! THAT'S A HANK'S ORIGINAL... ON 73RD STREET!
I'M COMING, CARLITOS!

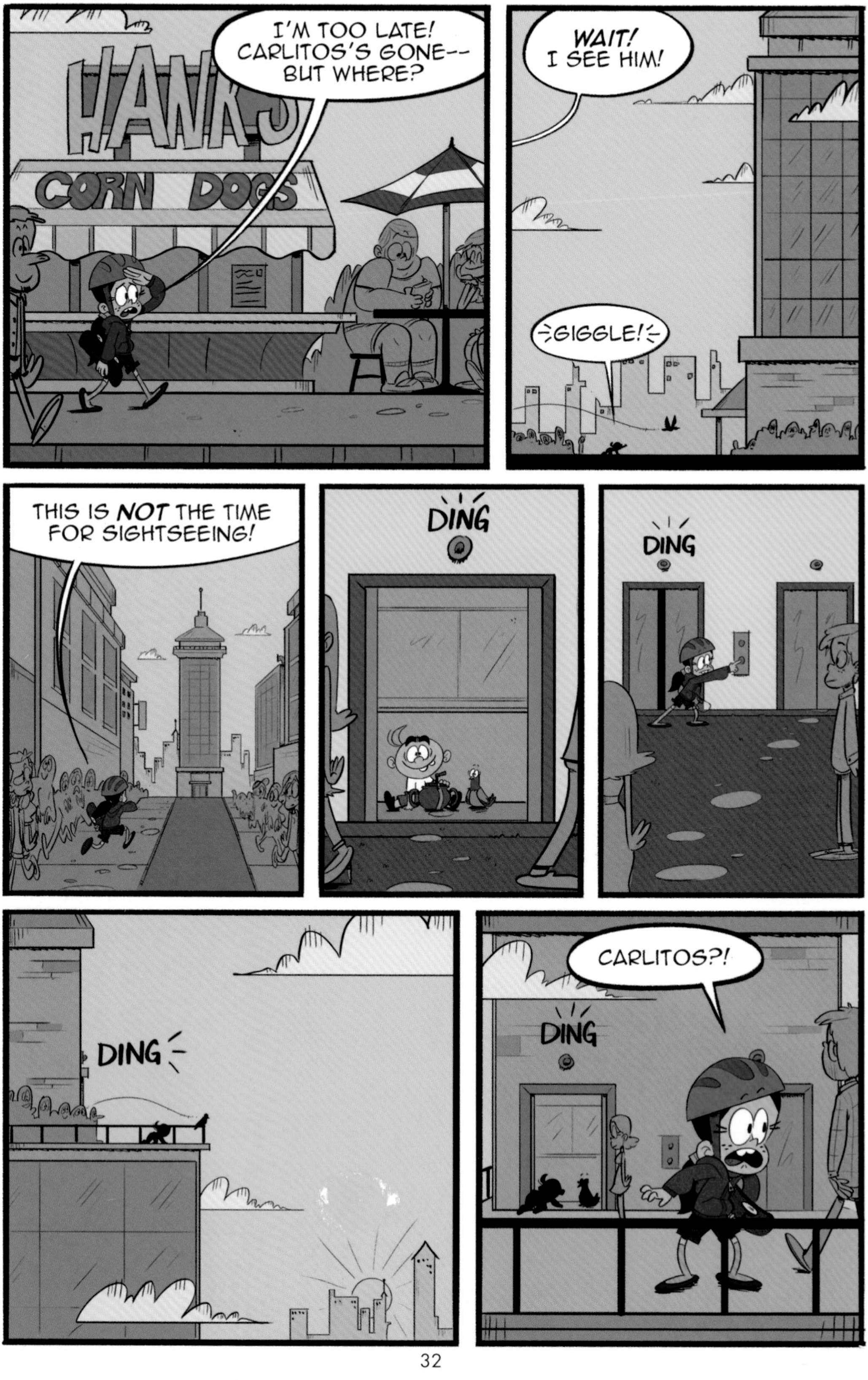
HANK'S
CORN DOGS
I'M TOO LATE! CARLITOS'S GONE-- BUT WHERE?
WAIT! I SEE HIM!
GIGGLE!
THIS IS NOT THE TIME FOR SIGHTSEEING!
DING
DING
DING
DING
CARLITOS?!

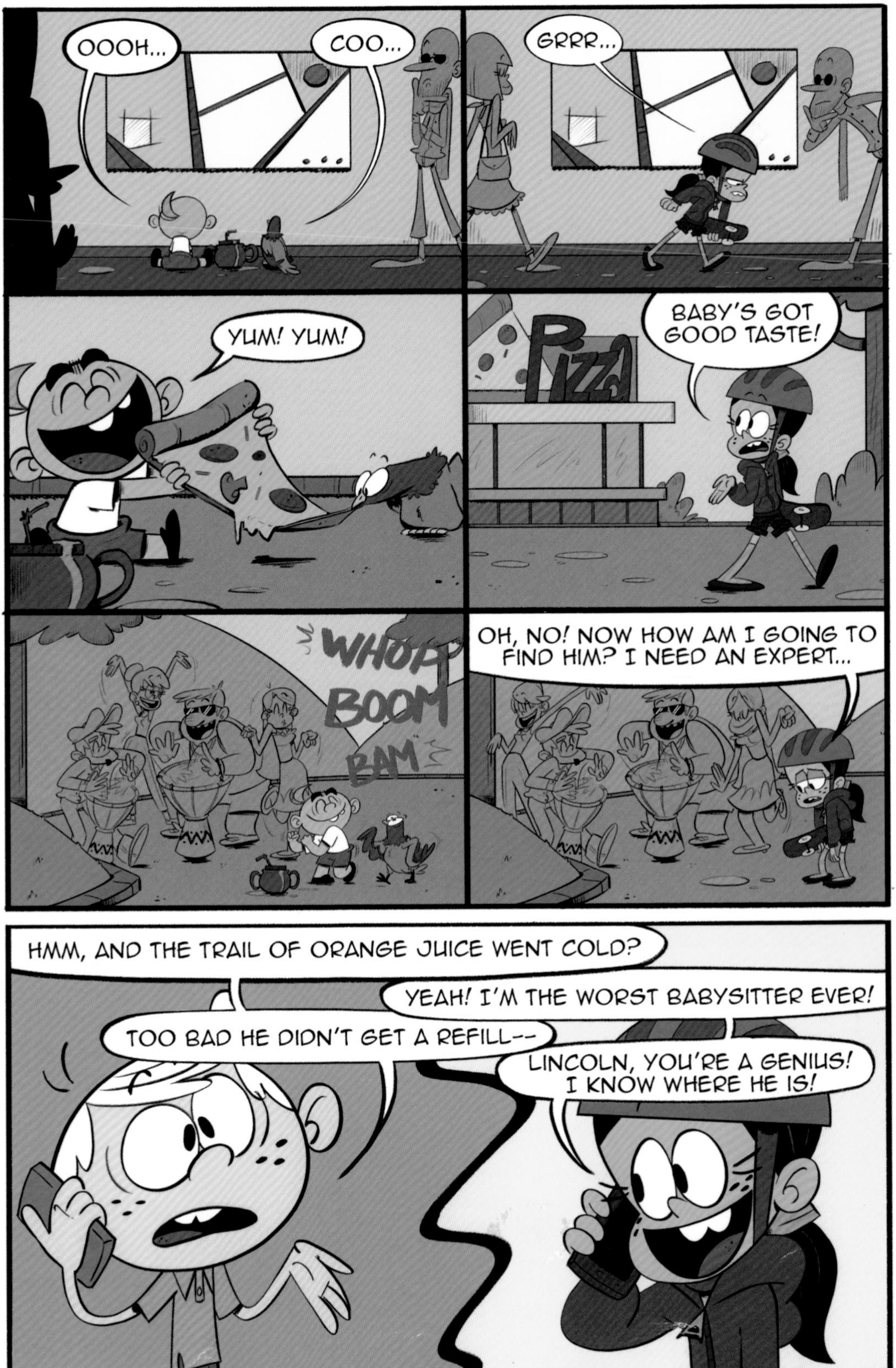
OOOH...
COO...
GRRR...
YUM! YUM!
BABY'S GOT GOOD TASTE!
WHOP
BOOM
BAM
OH, NO! NOW HOW AM I GOING TO FIND HIM? I NEED AN EXPERT...
HMM, AND THE TRAIL OF ORANGE JUICE WENT COLD?
YEAH! I'M THE WORST BABYSITTER EVER!
TOO BAD HE DIDN'T GET A REFILL--
LINCOLN, YOU'RE A GENIUS! I KNOW WHERE HE IS!

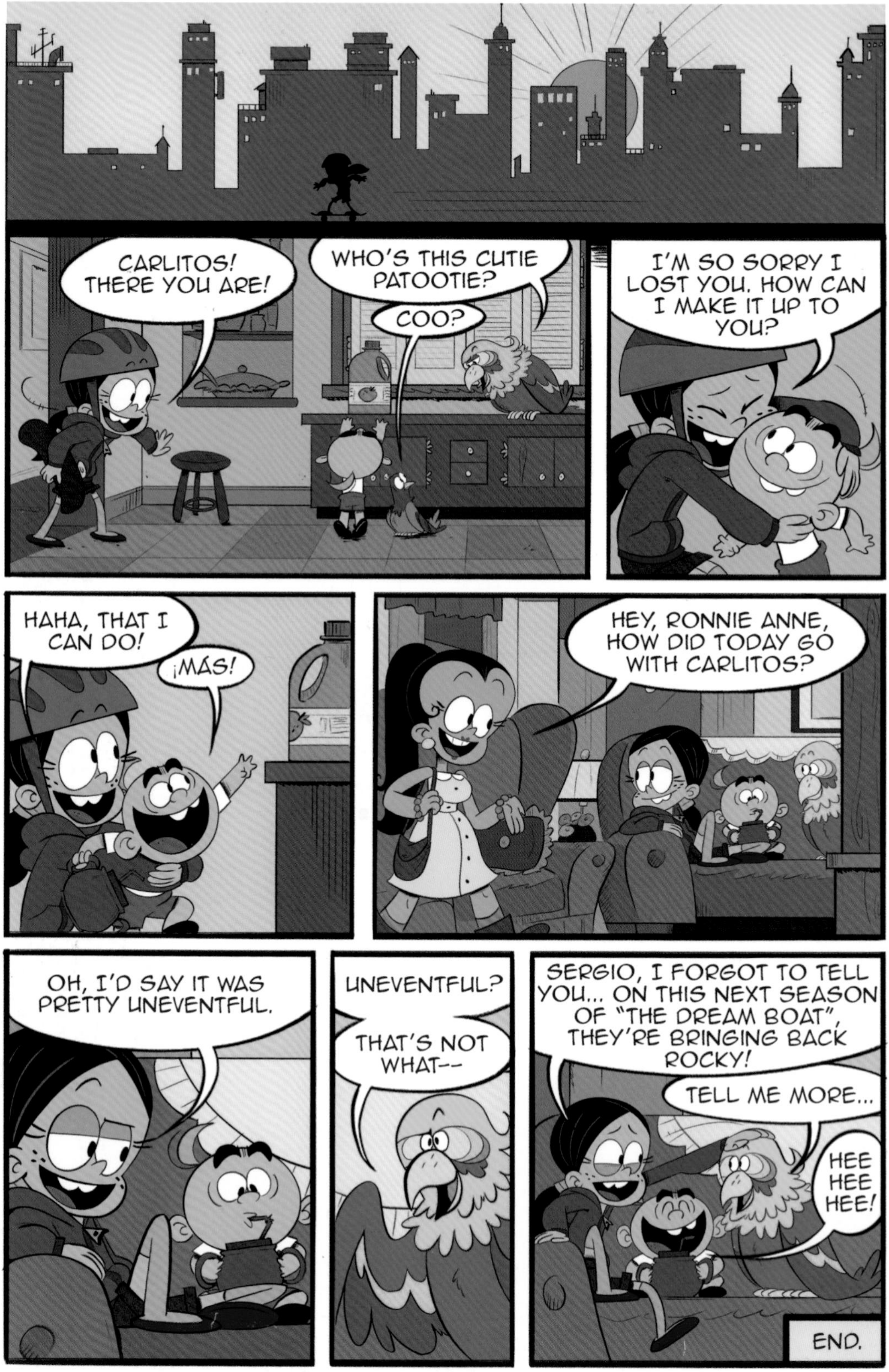
CARLITOS! THERE YOU ARE!
WHO'S THIS CUTIE PATOOTIE?
COO?
I'M SO SORRY I LOST YOU. HOW CAN I MAKE IT UP TO YOU?
HAHA, THAT I CAN DO!
¡MÁS!
HEY, RONNIE ANNE, HOW DID TODAY GO WITH CARLITOS?
OH, I'D SAY IT WAS PRETTY UNEVENTFUL.
UNEVENTFUL?
THAT'S NOT WHAT--
SERGIO, I FORGOT TO TELL YOU... ON THIS NEXT SEASON OF "THE DREAM BOAT", THEY'RE BRINGING BACK ROCKY!
TELL ME MORE...
HEE HEE HEE!
END.

"PACKING PARENTS"

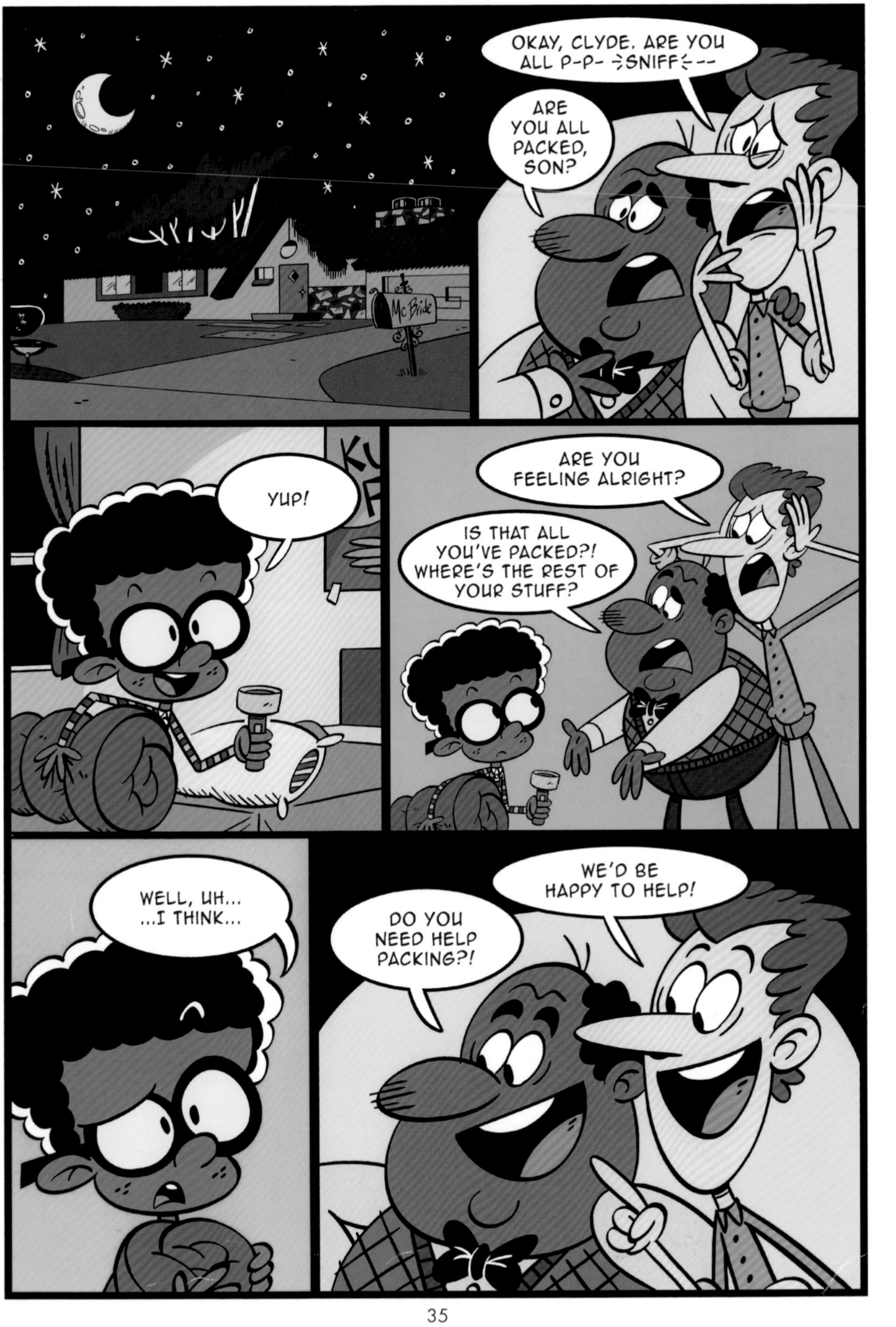
Mc Bride
OKAY, CLYDE. ARE YOU ALL P-P- ⇉SNIFF⇇--
ARE YOU ALL PACKED, SON?
YUP!
ARE YOU FEELING ALRIGHT?
IS THAT ALL YOU'VE PACKED?! WHERE'S THE REST OF YOUR STUFF?
WELL, UH... ...I THINK...
WE'D BE HAPPY TO HELP!
DO YOU NEED HELP PACKING?!

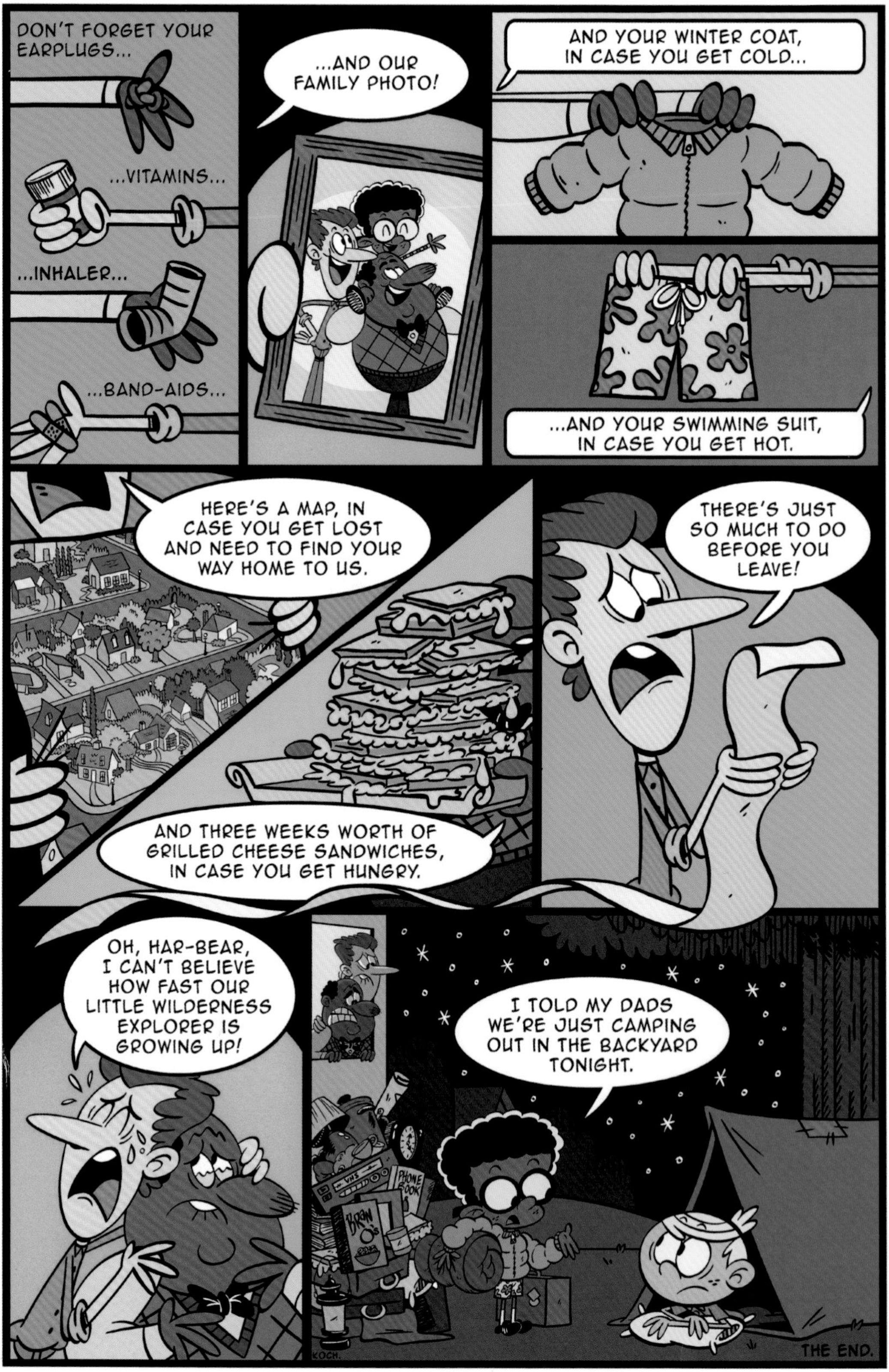
DON'T FORGET YOUR EARPLUGS...
...VITAMINS...
...INHALER...
...BAND-AIDS...
...AND OUR FAMILY PHOTO!
AND YOUR WINTER COAT, IN CASE YOU GET COLD...
...AND YOUR SWIMMING SUIT, IN CASE YOU GET HOT.
HERE'S A MAP, IN CASE YOU GET LOST AND NEED TO FIND YOUR WAY HOME TO US.
AND THREE WEEKS WORTH OF GRILLED CHEESE SANDWICHES, IN CASE YOU GET HUNGRY.
THERE'S JUST SO MUCH TO DO BEFORE YOU LEAVE!
OH, HAR-BEAR, I CAN'T BELIEVE HOW FAST OUR LITTLE WILDERNESS EXPLORER IS GROWING UP!
I TOLD MY DADS WE'RE JUST CAMPING OUT IN THE BACKYARD TONIGHT.
PHONE BOOK
BRAN O's
KOCH.
THE END.

"IT'S JUST A PHASE"

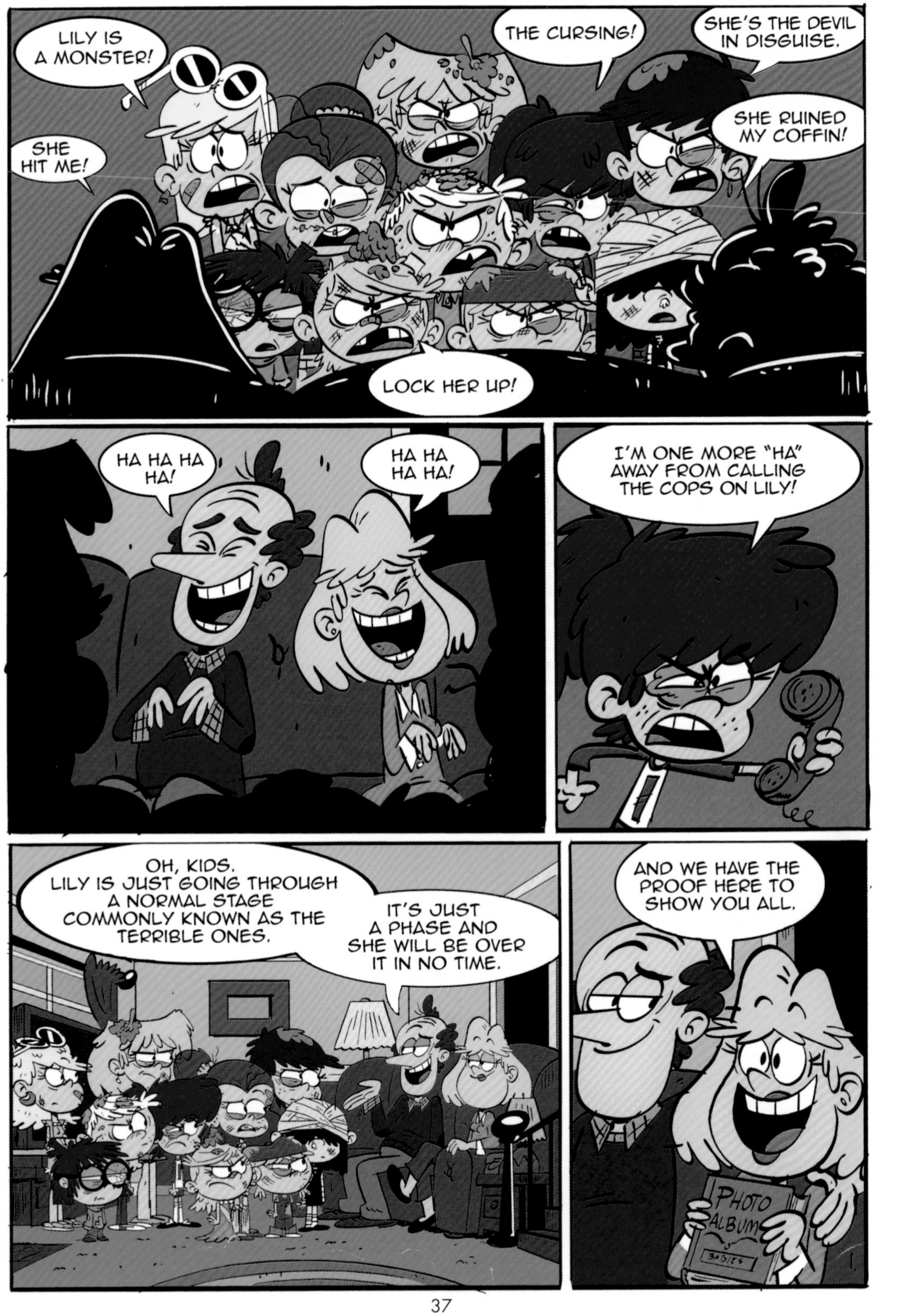
LILY IS A MONSTER!
THE CURSING!
SHE'S THE DEVIL IN DISGUISE.
SHE HIT ME!
SHE RUINED MY COFFIN!
LOCK HER UP!
HA HA HA HA!
HA HA HA HA!
I'M ONE MORE "HA" AWAY FROM CALLING THE COPS ON LILY!
OH, KIDS. LILY IS JUST GOING THROUGH A NORMAL STAGE COMMONLY KNOWN AS THE TERRIBLE ONES.
IT'S JUST A PHASE AND SHE WILL BE OVER IT IN NO TIME.
AND WE HAVE THE PROOF HERE TO SHOW YOU ALL.
PHOTO ALBUM
BABIES

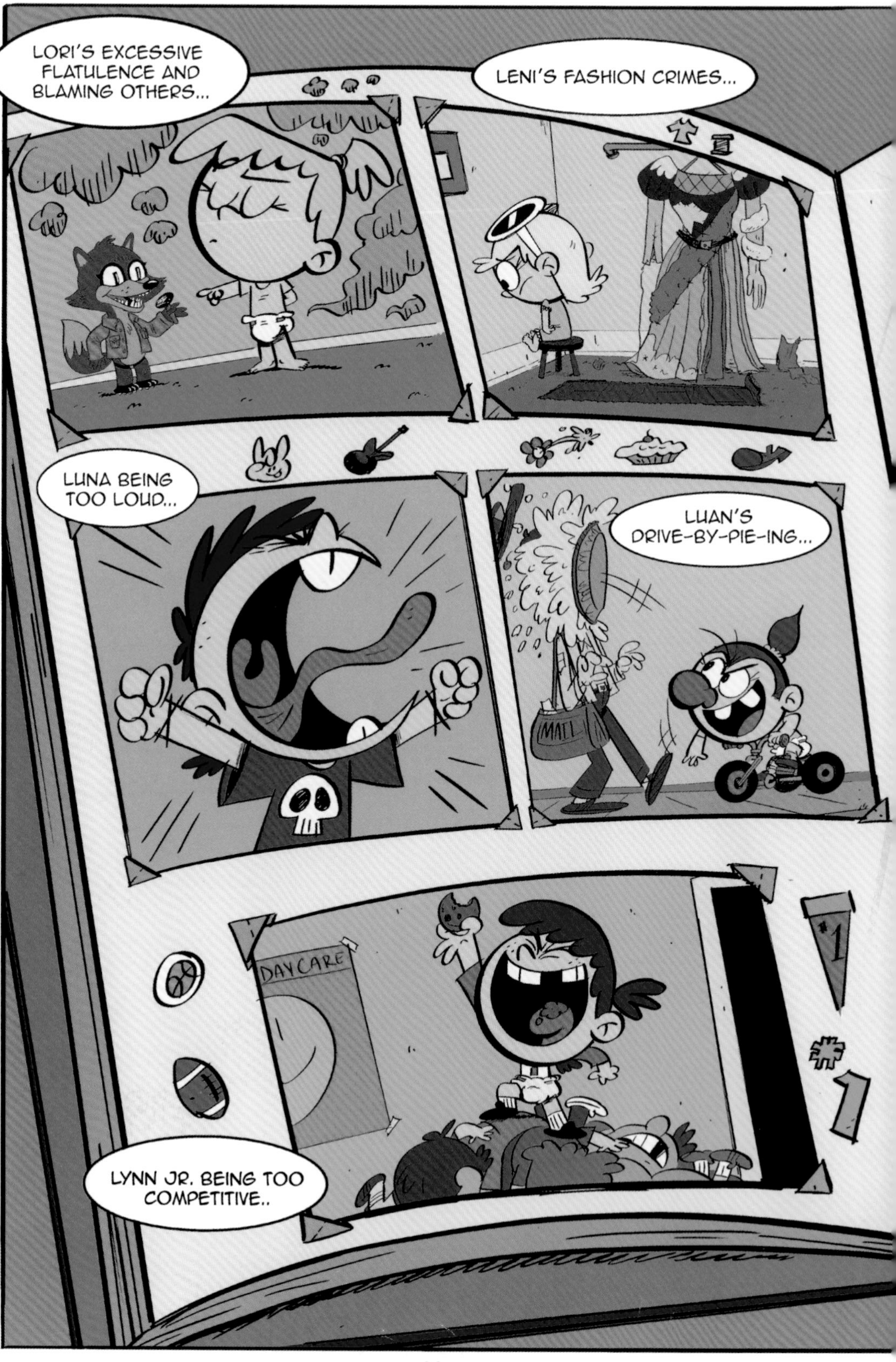
LORI'S EXCESSIVE FLATULENCE AND BLAMING OTHERS...
LENI'S FASHION CRIMES...
LUNA BEING TOO LOUD...
LUAN'S DRIVE-BY-PIE-ING...
MAIL
DAYCARE
#1
#1
LYNN JR. BEING TOO COMPETITIVE..

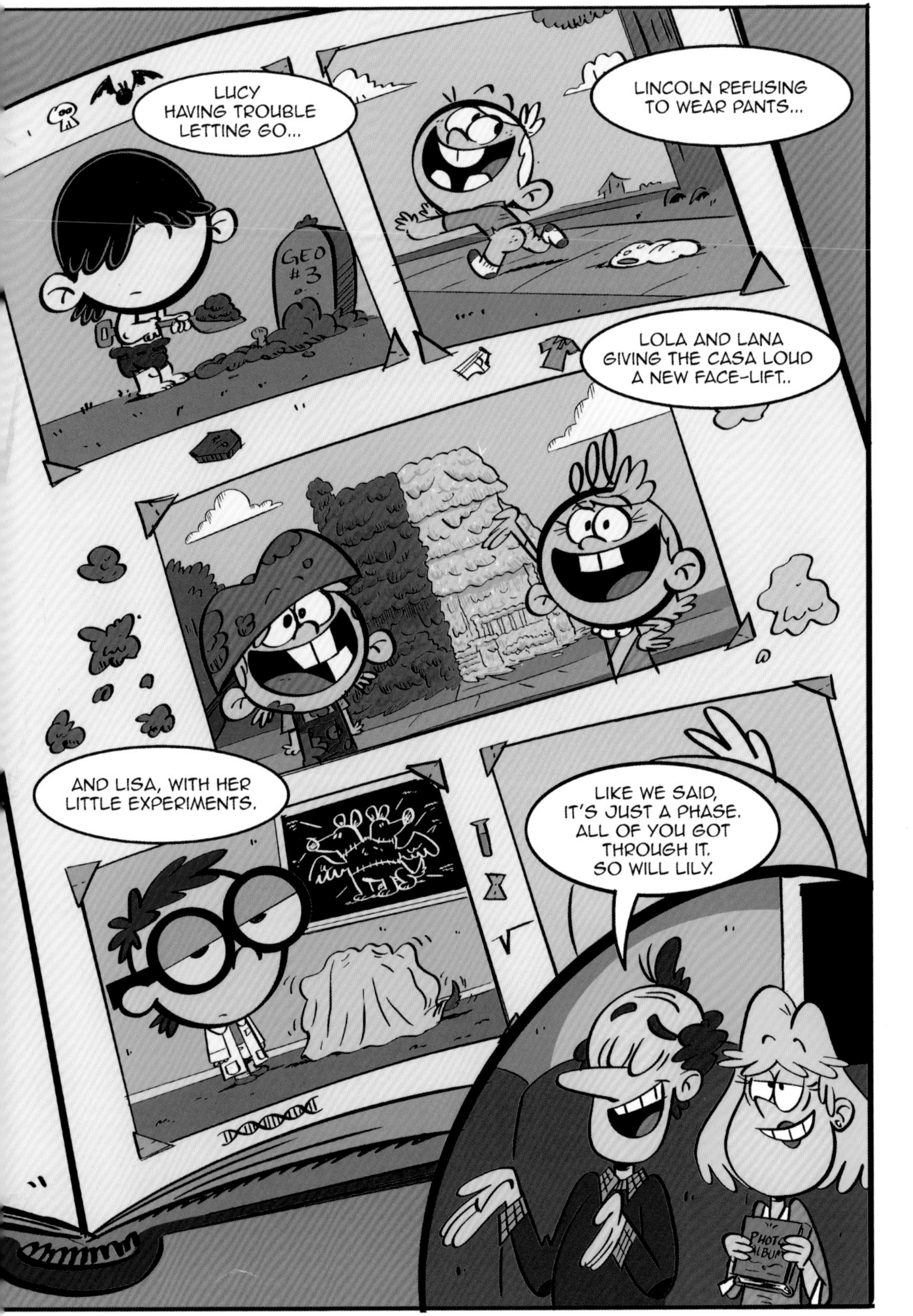
LUCY HAVING TROUBLE LETTING GO...
GEO #3
LINCOLN REFUSING TO WEAR PANTS...
LOLA AND LANA GIVING THE CASA LOUD A NEW FACE-LIFT..
AND LISA, WITH HER LITTLE EXPERIMENTS.
LIKE WE SAID, IT'S JUST A PHASE. ALL OF YOU GOT THROUGH IT. SO WILL LILY.
PHOTO ALBUM

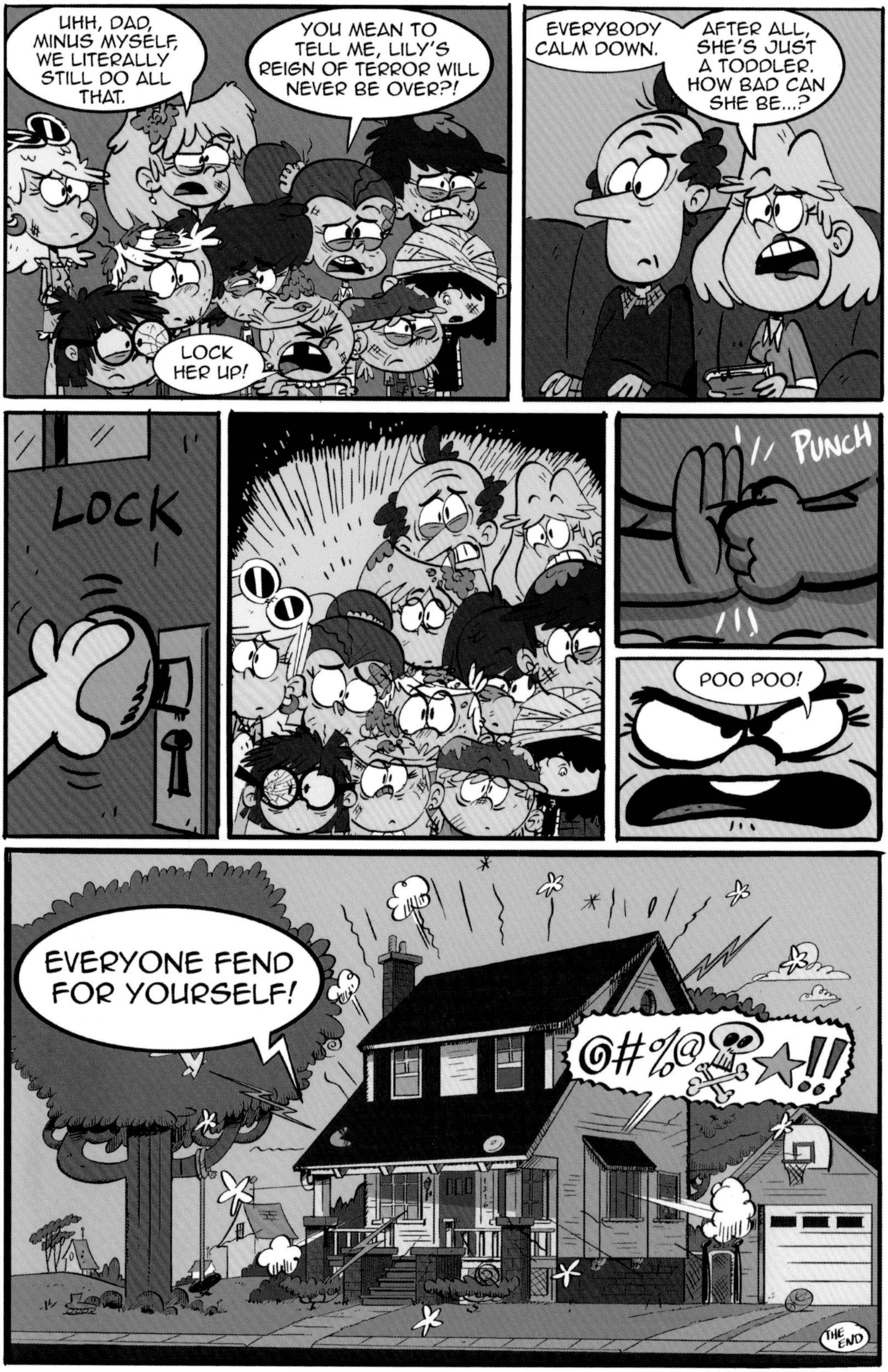
UHH, DAD, MINUS MYSELF, WE LITERALLY STILL DO ALL THAT.
YOU MEAN TO TELL ME, LILY'S REIGN OF TERROR WILL NEVER BE OVER?!
LOCK HER UP!
EVERYBODY CALM DOWN.
AFTER ALL, SHE'S JUST A TODDLER. HOW BAD CAN SHE BE...?
LOCK
PUNCH
POO POO!
EVERYONE FEND FOR YOURSELF!
@#%@
THE END

"LOST AND FOUND"

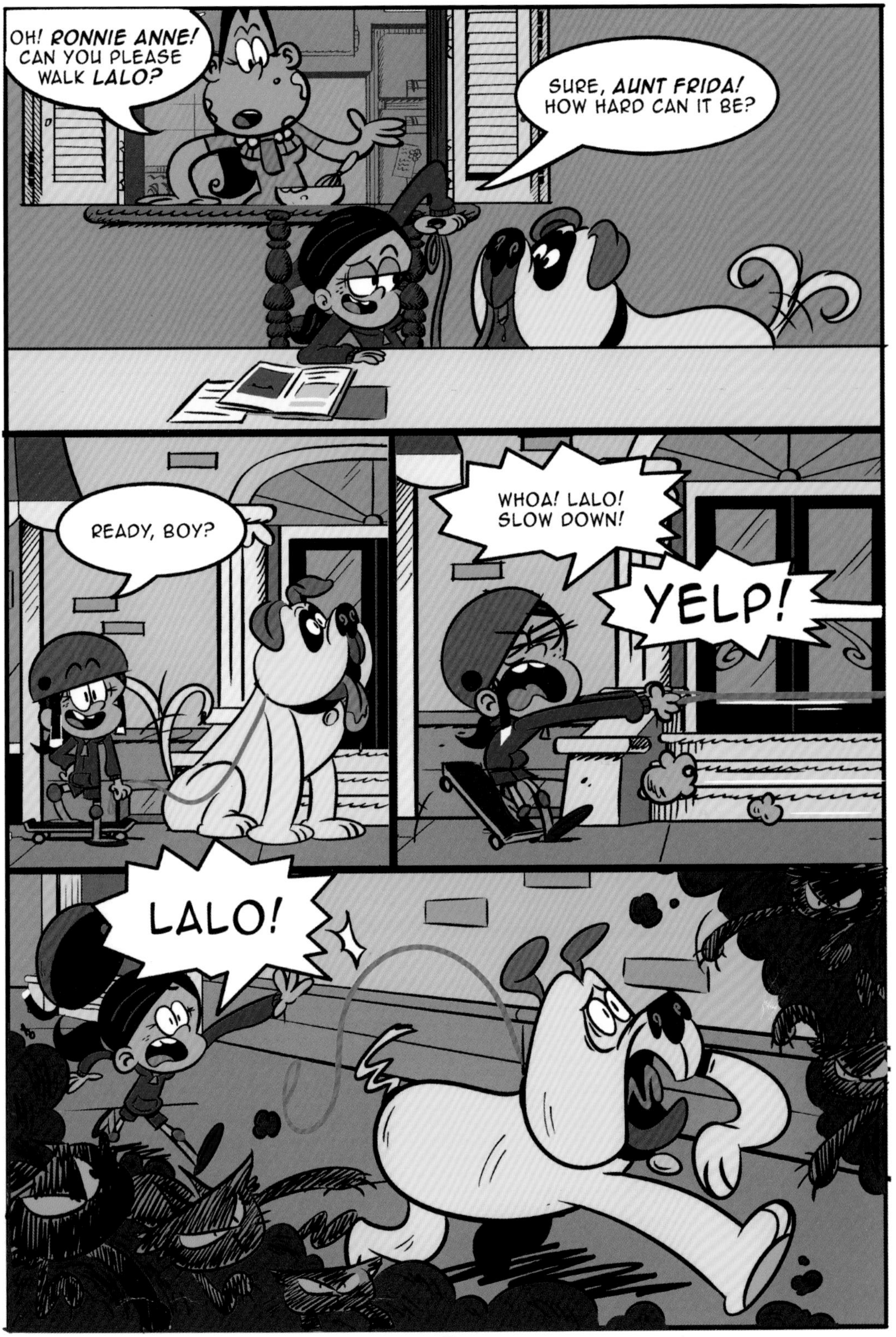

OH! RONNIE ANNE! CAN YOU PLEASE WALK LALO?
SURE, AUNT FRIDA! HOW HARD CAN IT BE?
READY, BOY?
WHOA! LALO! SLOW DOWN!
YELP!
LALO!

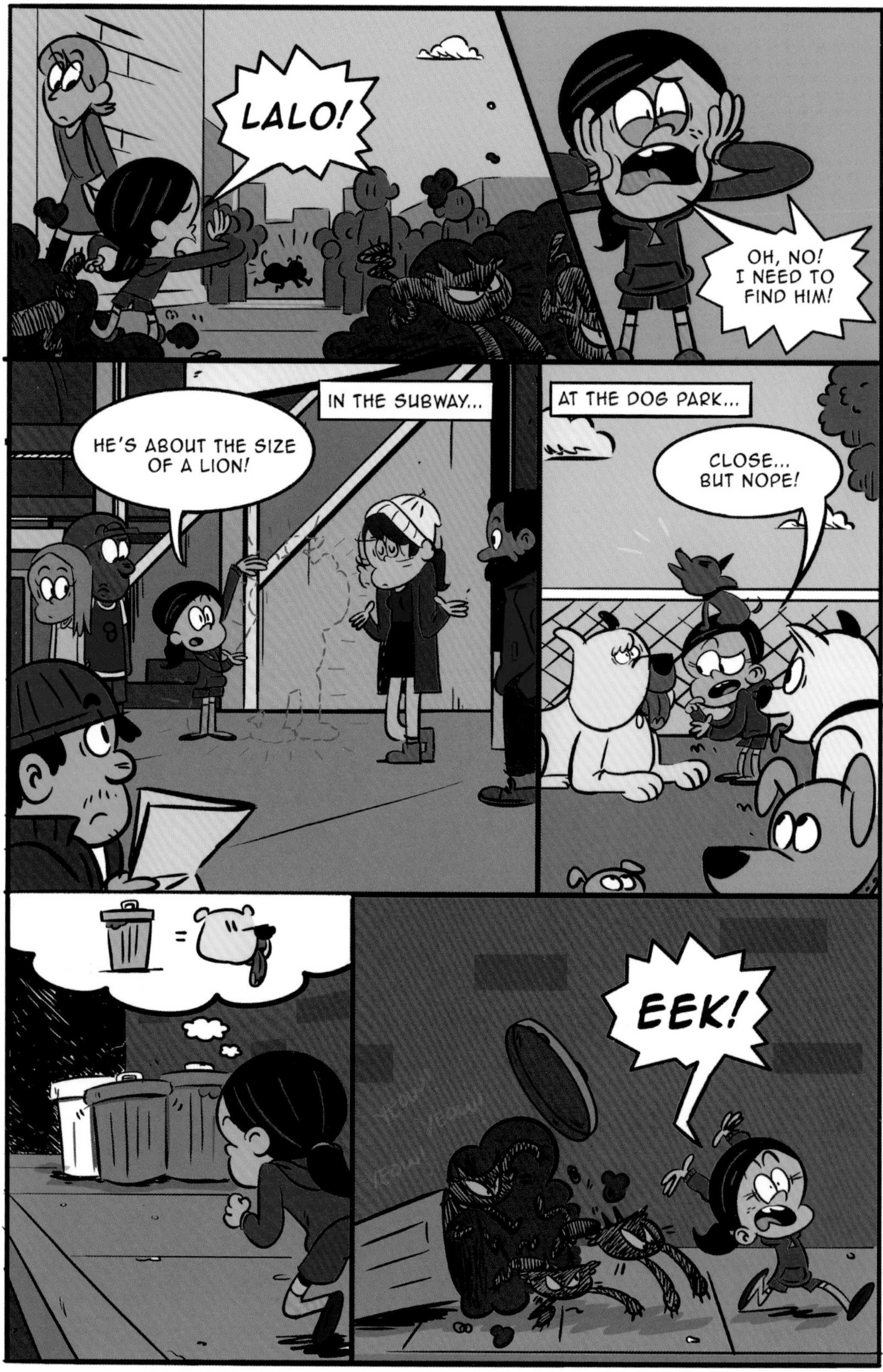
LALO!
OH, NO! I NEED TO FIND HIM!
IN THE SUBWAY...
HE'S ABOUT THE SIZE OF A LION!
AT THE DOG PARK...
CLOSE... BUT NOPE!
EEK!

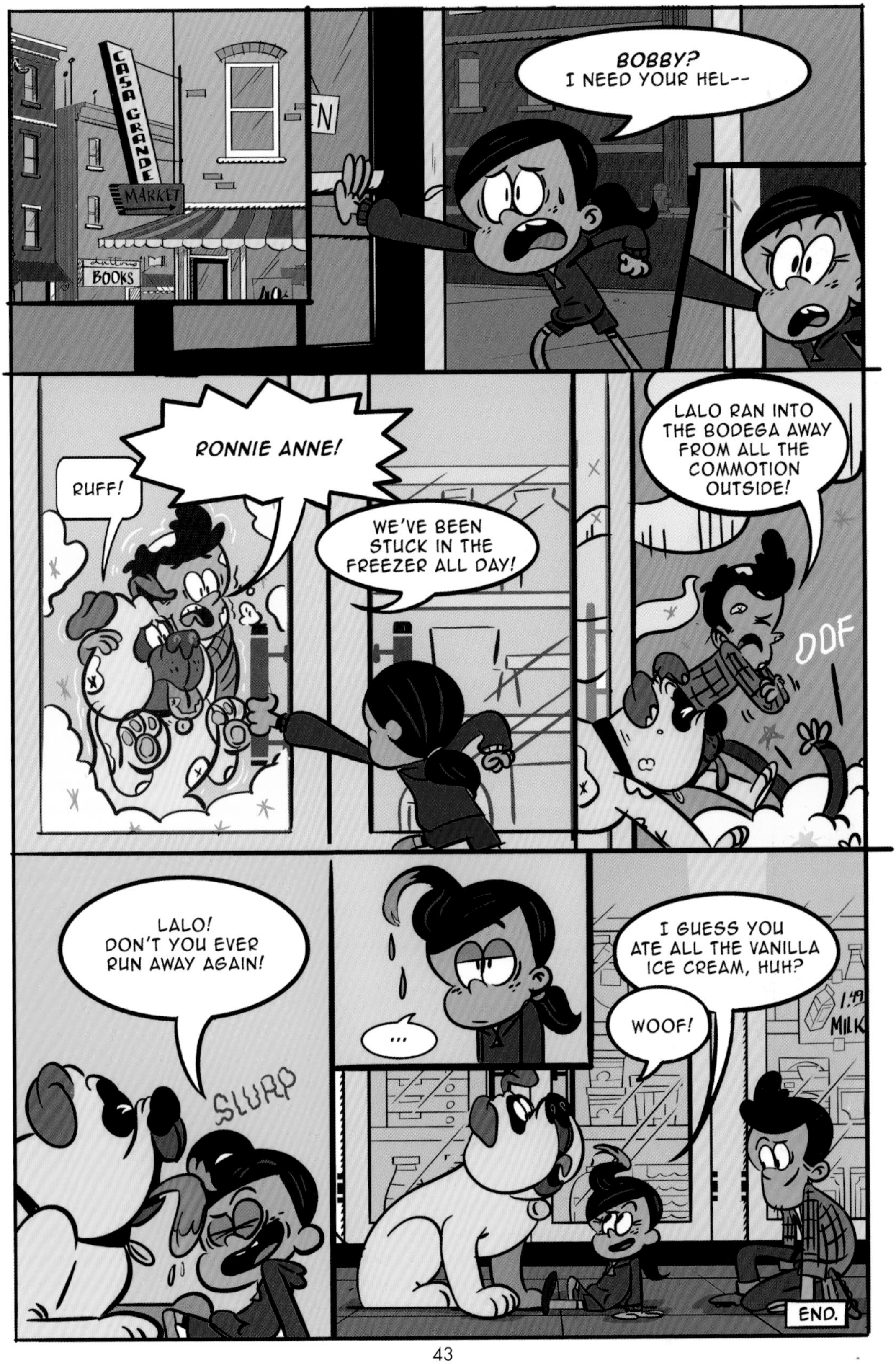
CASA GRANDE
MARKET
BOOKS
BOBBY? I NEED YOUR HEL--
RUFF!
RONNIE ANNE!
WE'VE BEEN STUCK IN THE FREEZER ALL DAY!
LALO RAN INTO THE BODEGA AWAY FROM ALL THE COMMOTION OUTSIDE!
OOF
LALO! DON'T YOU EVER RUN AWAY AGAIN!
SLURP
...
I GUESS YOU ATE ALL THE VANILLA ICE CREAM, HUH?
WOOF!
MILK
END.

"I SPY LASAGNA"

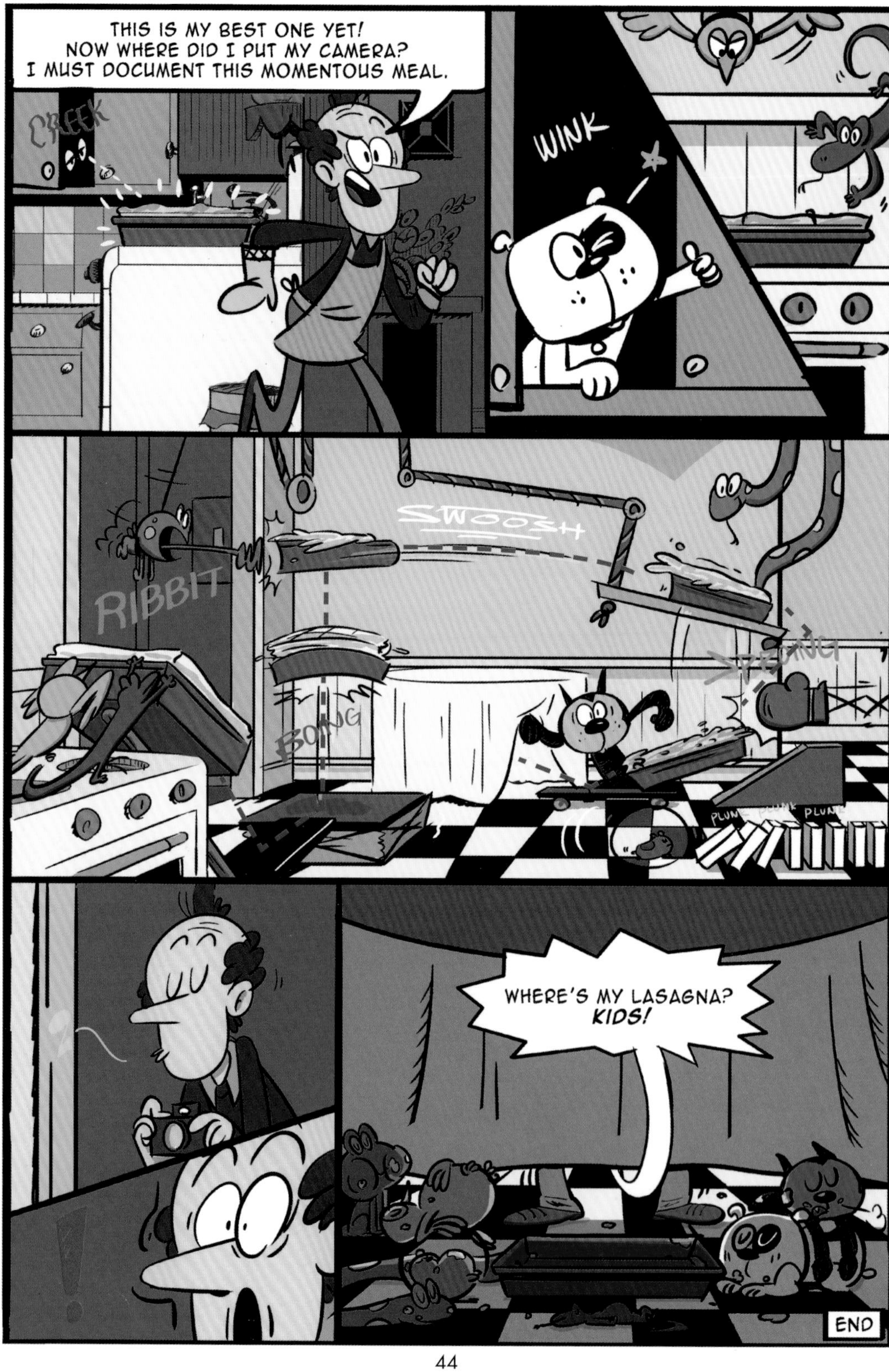
THIS IS MY BEST ONE YET!
NOW WHERE DID I PUT MY CAMERA?
I MUST DOCUMENT THIS MOMENTOUS MEAL.
CREEK
WINK
SWOOSH
RIBBIT
BOING
SPROING
PLUNK PLUNK PLUNK
WHERE'S MY LASAGNA?
KIDS!
END

"SAM'S PICK"

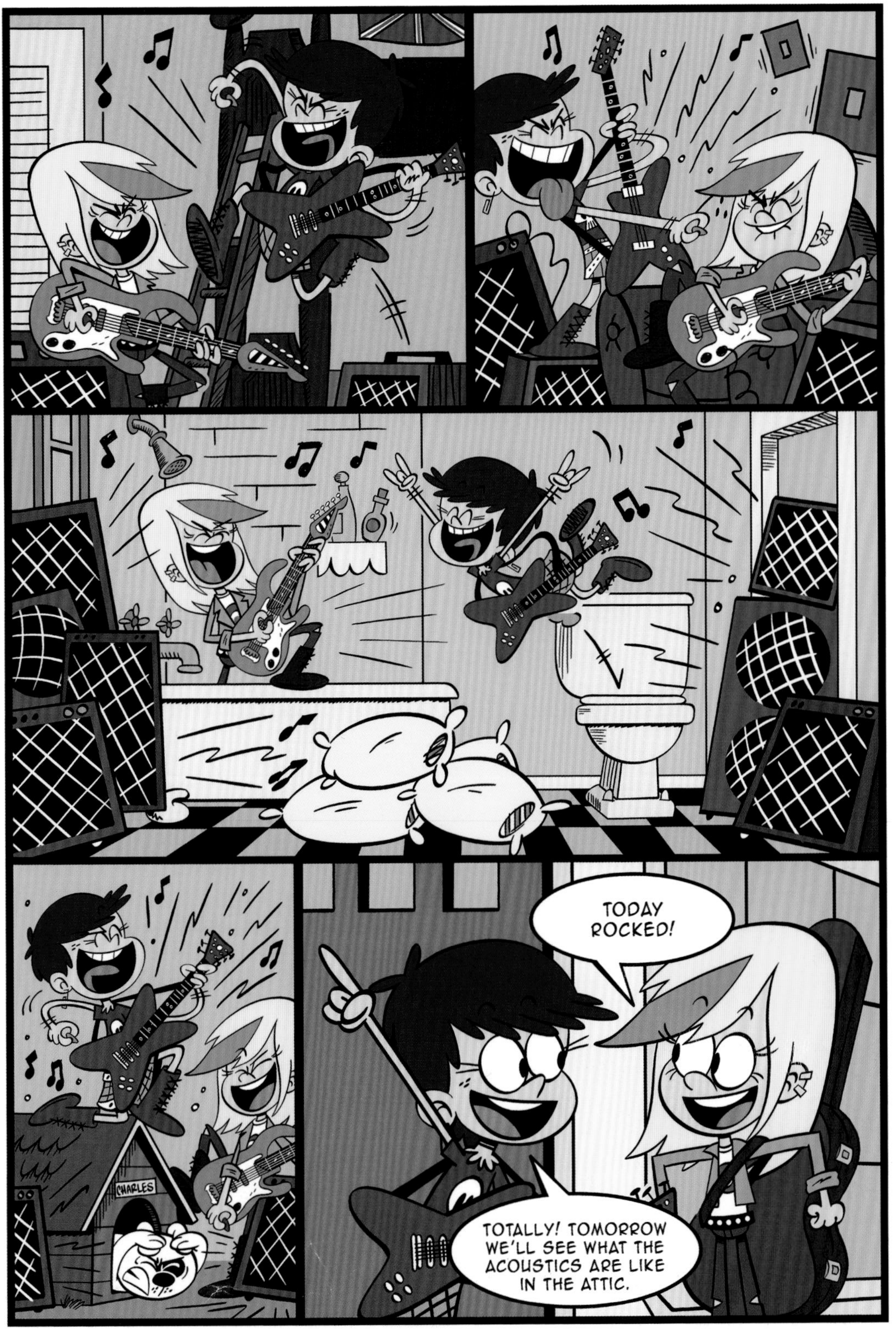

CHARLES
TODAY ROCKED!
TOTALLY! TOMORROW WE'LL SEE WHAT THE ACOUSTICS ARE LIKE IN THE ATTIC.

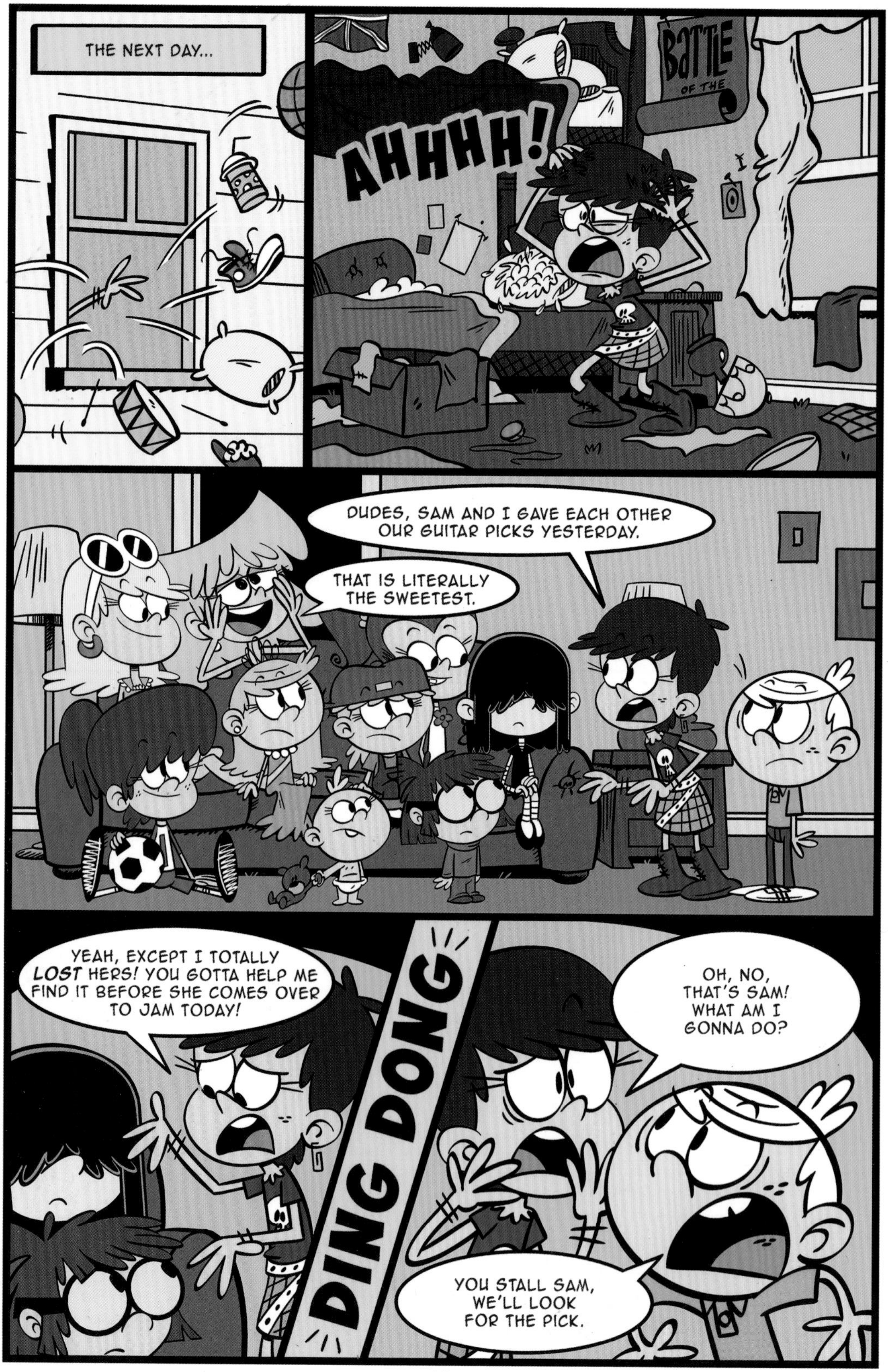
THE NEXT DAY...
AHHHH!
BATTLE OF THE
DUDES, SAM AND I GAVE EACH OTHER OUR GUITAR PICKS YESTERDAY.
THAT IS LITERALLY THE SWEETEST.
YEAH, EXCEPT I TOTALLY *LOST* HERS! YOU GOTTA HELP ME FIND IT BEFORE SHE COMES OVER TO JAM TODAY!
DING DONG
OH, NO, THAT'S SAM! WHAT AM I GONNA DO?
YOU STALL SAM, WE'LL LOOK FOR THE PICK.

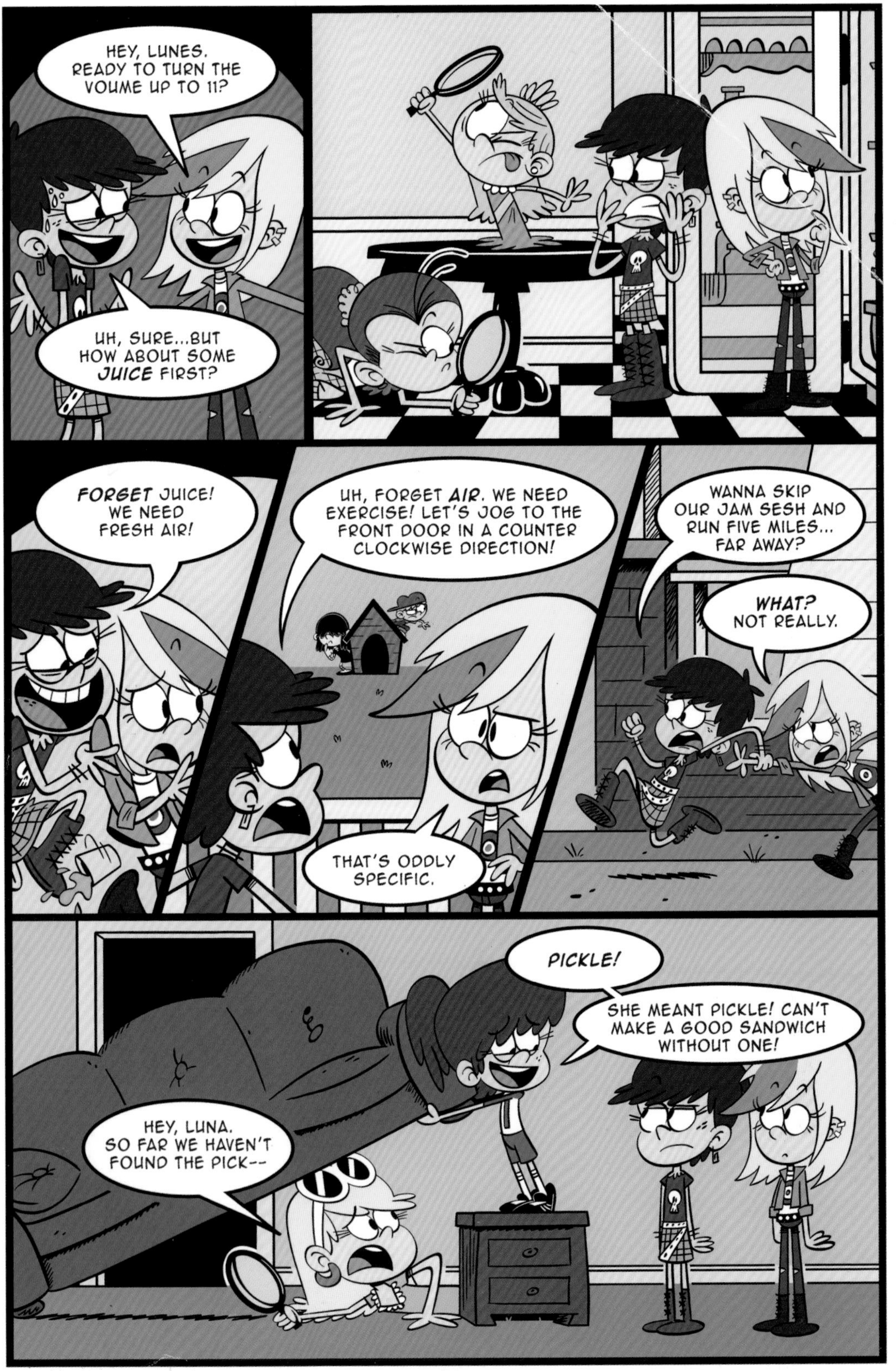
HEY, LUNES. READY TO TURN THE VOUME UP TO 11?
UH, SURE...BUT HOW ABOUT SOME *JUICE* FIRST?
FORGET JUICE! WE NEED FRESH AIR!
UH, FORGET *AIR*. WE NEED EXERCISE! LET'S JOG TO THE FRONT DOOR IN A COUNTER CLOCKWISE DIRECTION!
THAT'S ODDLY SPECIFIC.
WANNA SKIP OUR JAM SESH AND RUN FIVE MILES... FAR AWAY?
WHAT? NOT REALLY.
PICKLE!
SHE MEANT PICKLE! CAN'T MAKE A GOOD SANDWICH WITHOUT ONE!
HEY, LUNA. SO FAR WE HAVEN'T FOUND THE PICK--

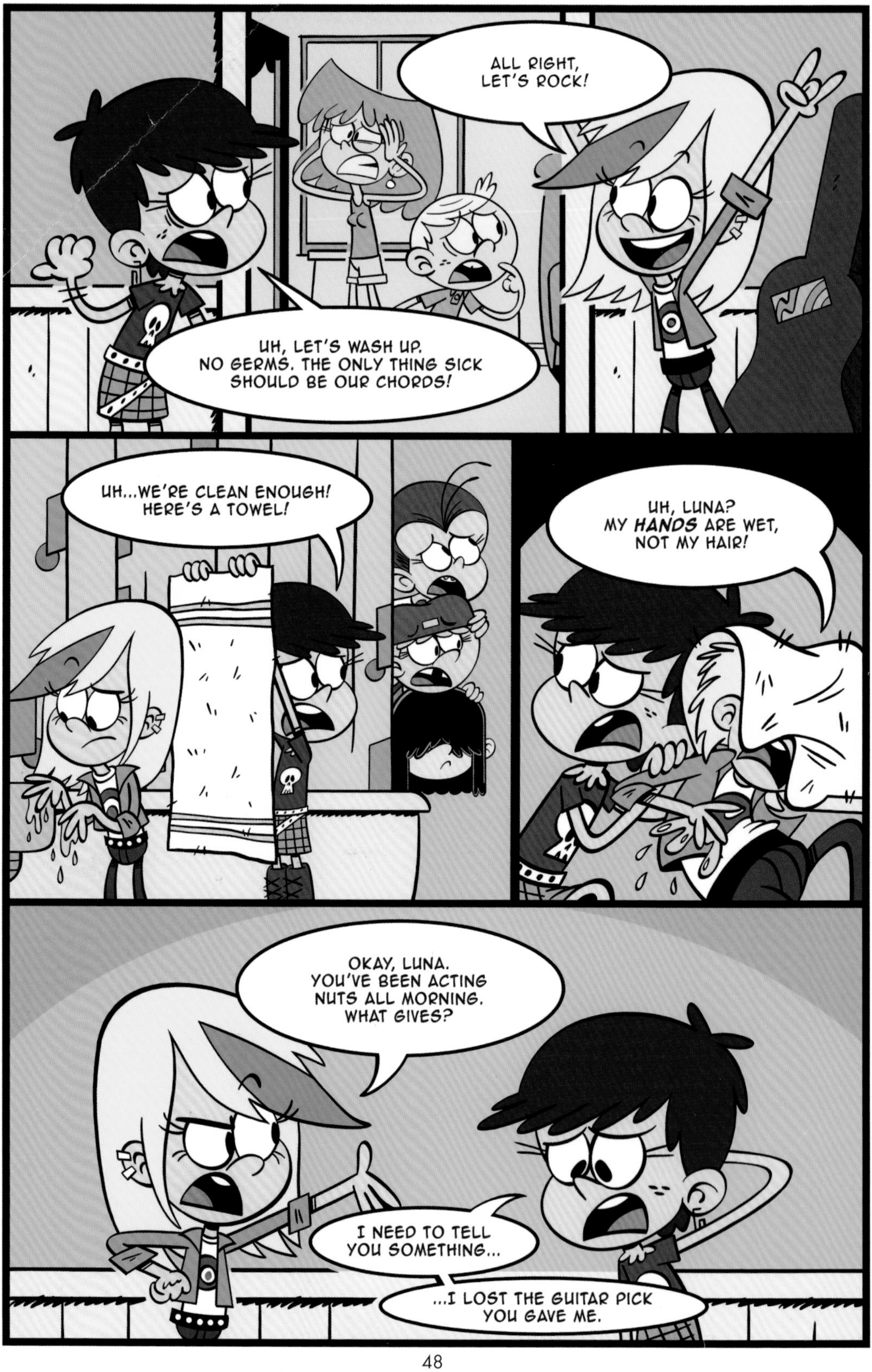
ALL RIGHT, LET'S ROCK!
UH, LET'S WASH UP. NO GERMS. THE ONLY THING SICK SHOULD BE OUR CHORDS!
UH...WE'RE CLEAN ENOUGH! HERE'S A TOWEL!
UH, LUNA? MY **HANDS** ARE WET, NOT MY HAIR!
OKAY, LUNA. YOU'VE BEEN ACTING NUTS ALL MORNING. WHAT GIVES?
I NEED TO TELL YOU SOMETHING...
...I LOST THE GUITAR PICK YOU GAVE ME.

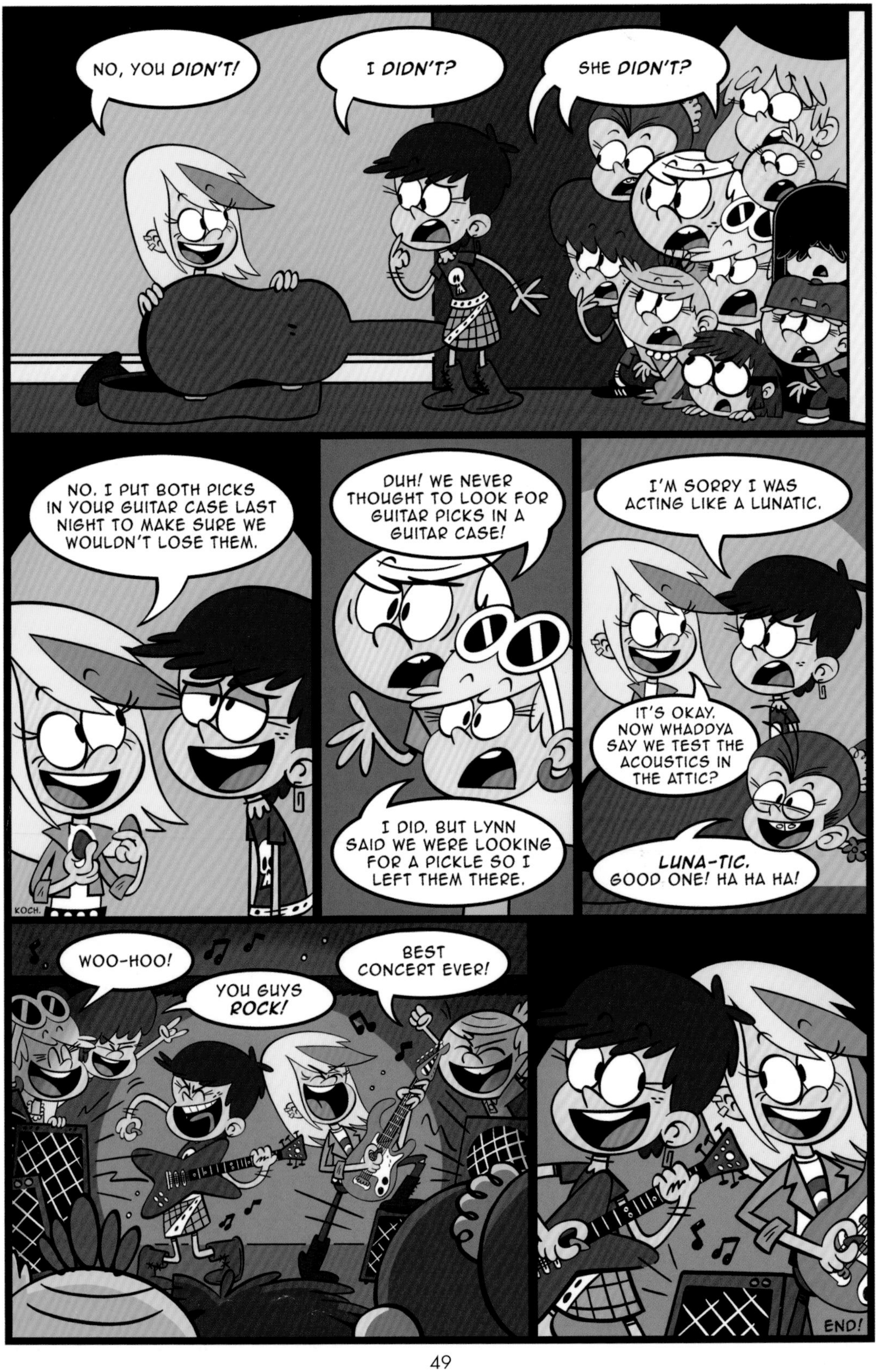
NO, YOU *DIDN'T!*
I *DIDN'T?*
SHE *DIDN'T?*
NO. I PUT BOTH PICKS IN YOUR GUITAR CASE LAST NIGHT TO MAKE SURE WE WOULDN'T LOSE THEM.
KOCH.
DUH! WE NEVER THOUGHT TO LOOK FOR GUITAR PICKS IN A GUITAR CASE!
I DID. BUT LYNN SAID WE WERE LOOKING FOR A PICKLE SO I LEFT THEM THERE.
I'M SORRY I WAS ACTING LIKE A LUNATIC.
IT'S OKAY. NOW WHADDYA SAY WE TEST THE ACOUSTICS IN THE ATTIC?
LUNA-TIC. GOOD ONE! HA HA HA!
WOO-HOO!
YOU GUYS *ROCK!*
BEST CONCERT EVER!
END!

"SHARE BEARS"

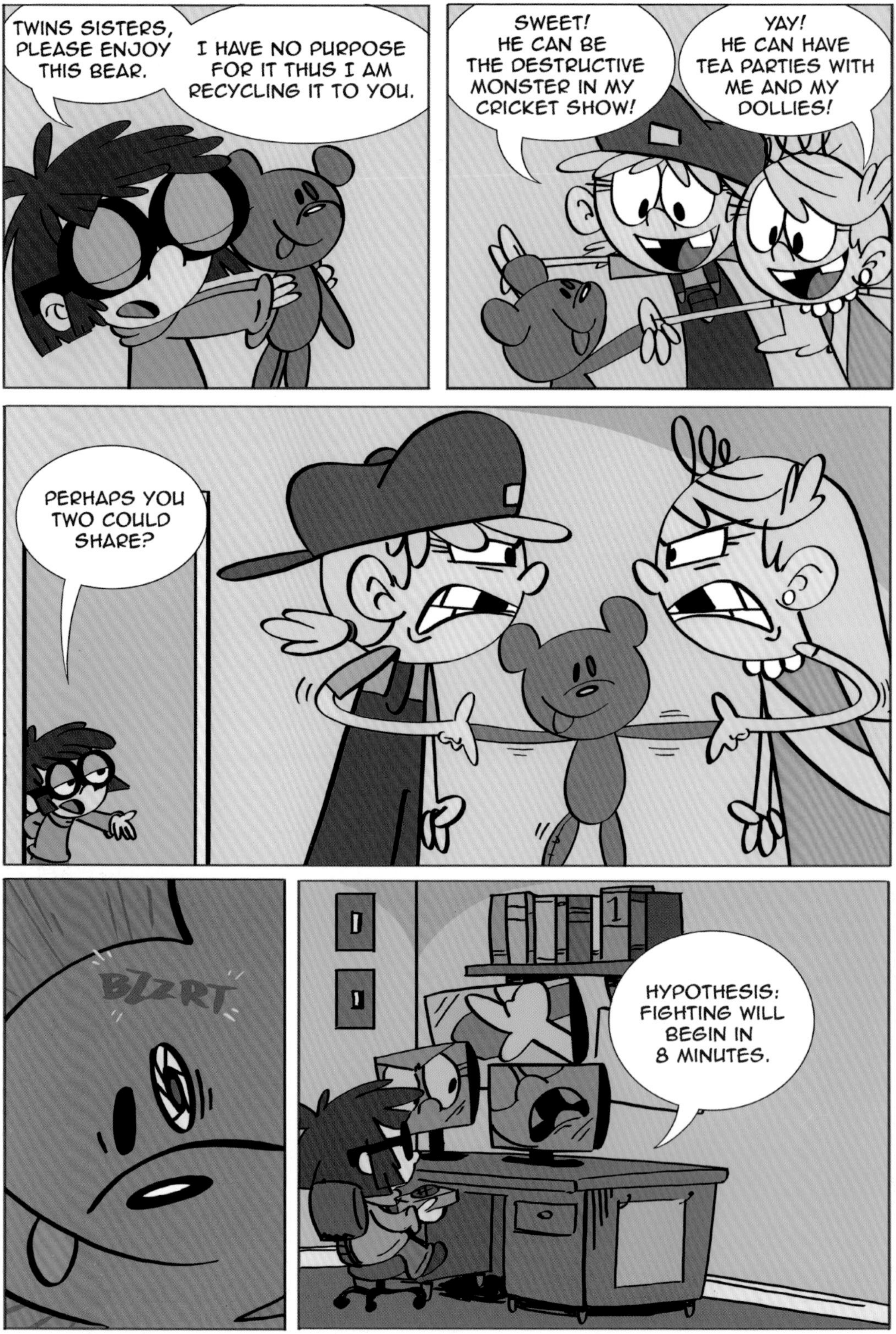
TWINS SISTERS, PLEASE ENJOY THIS BEAR.
I HAVE NO PURPOSE FOR IT THUS I AM RECYCLING IT TO YOU.
SWEET! HE CAN BE THE DESTRUCTIVE MONSTER IN MY CRICKET SHOW!
YAY! HE CAN HAVE TEA PARTIES WITH ME AND MY DOLLIES!
PERHAPS YOU TWO COULD SHARE?
BZZRT
HYPOTHESIS: FIGHTING WILL BEGIN IN 8 MINUTES.

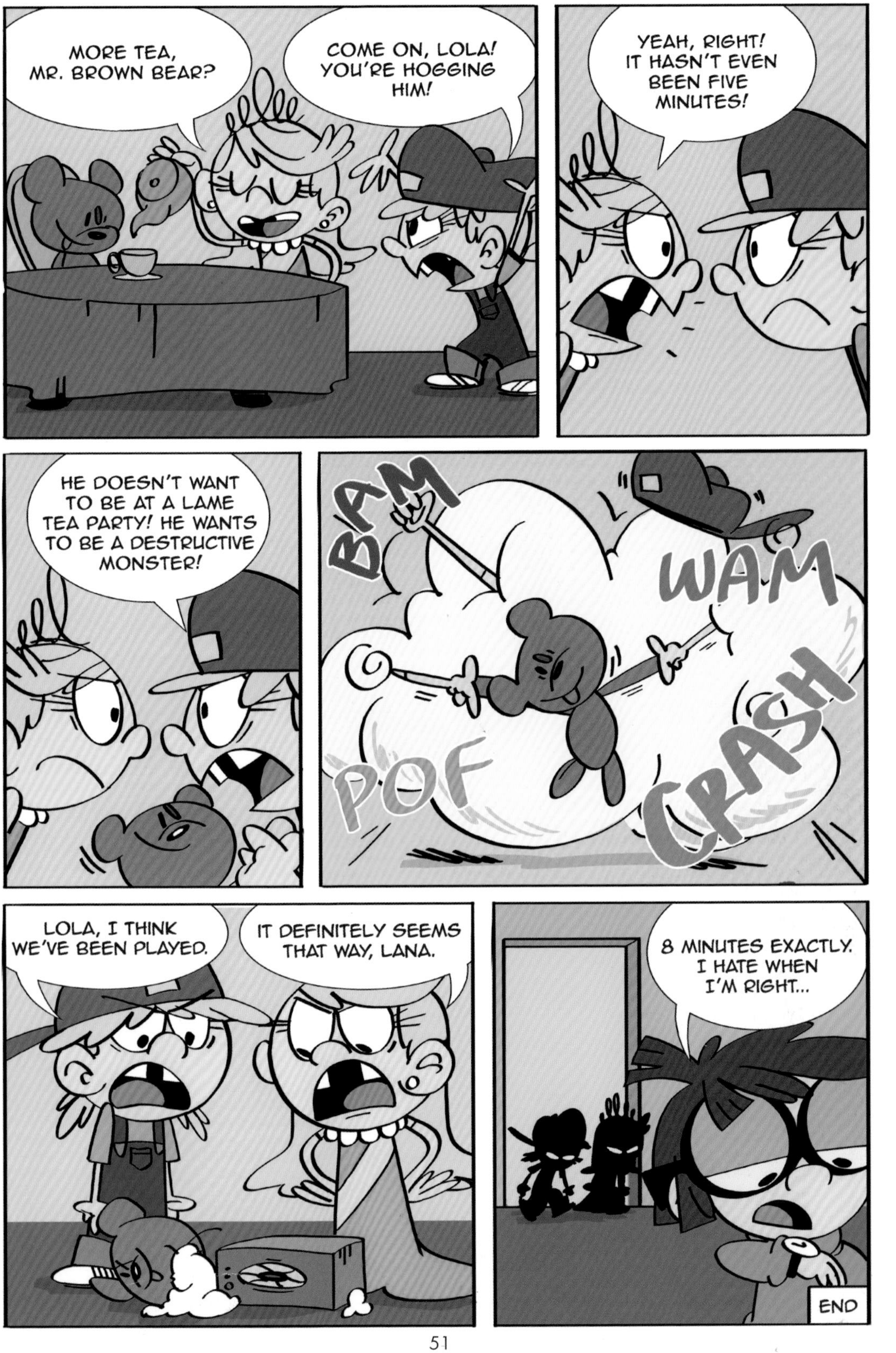
MORE TEA, MR. BROWN BEAR?
COME ON, LOLA! YOU'RE HOGGING HIM!
YEAH, RIGHT! IT HASN'T EVEN BEEN FIVE MINUTES!
HE DOESN'T WANT TO BE AT A LAME TEA PARTY! HE WANTS TO BE A DESTRUCTIVE MONSTER!
BAM
WAM
CRASH
POF
LOLA, I THINK WE'VE BEEN PLAYED.
IT DEFINITELY SEEMS THAT WAY, LANA.
8 MINUTES EXACTLY. I HATE WHEN I'M RIGHT...
END

"HELP WANTED"

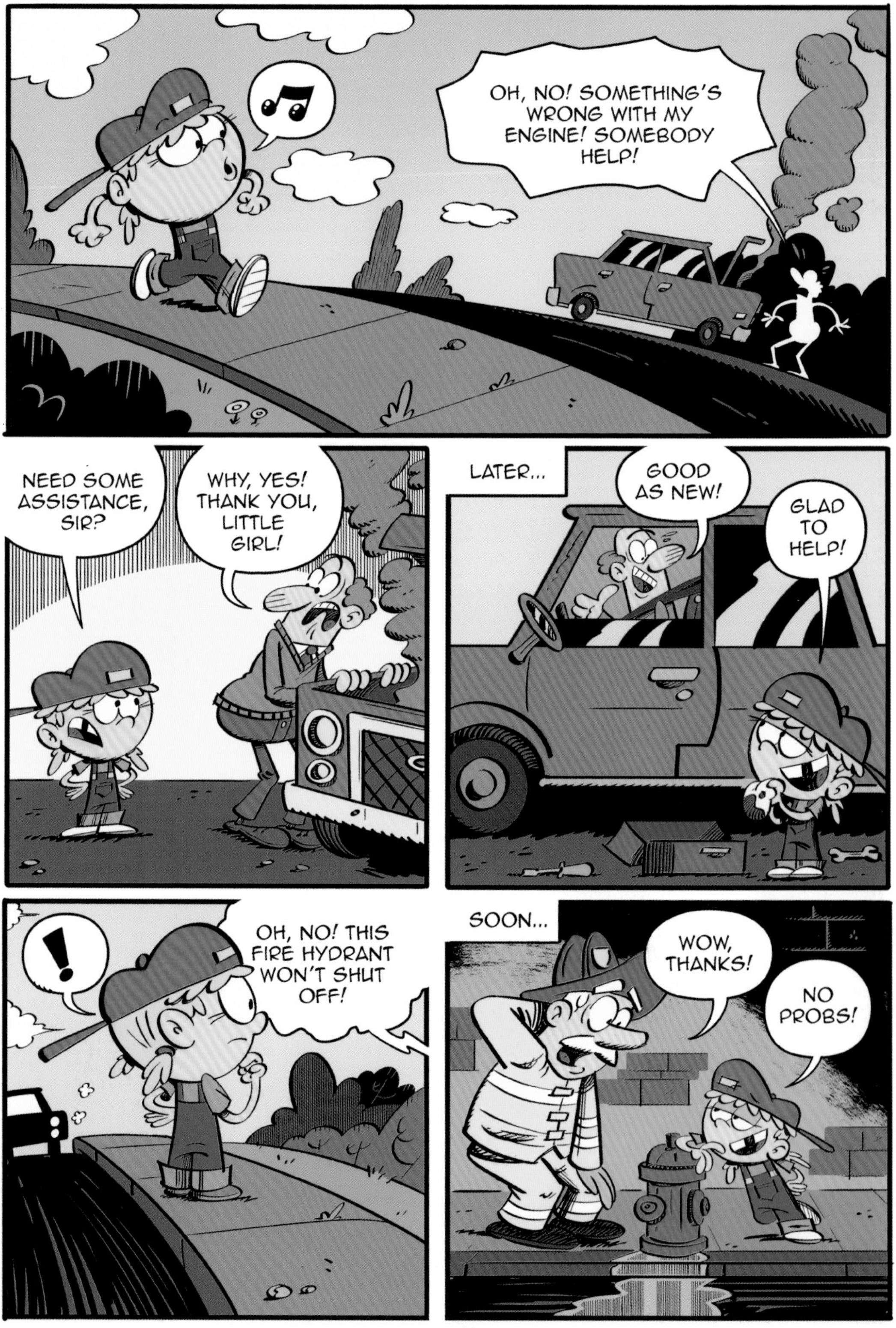

OH, NO! SOMETHING'S WRONG WITH MY ENGINE! SOMEBODY HELP!
NEED SOME ASSISTANCE, SIR?
WHY, YES! THANK YOU, LITTLE GIRL!
LATER...
GOOD AS NEW!
GLAD TO HELP!
!
OH, NO! THIS FIRE HYDRANT WON'T SHUT OFF!
SOON...
WOW, THANKS!
NO PROBS!

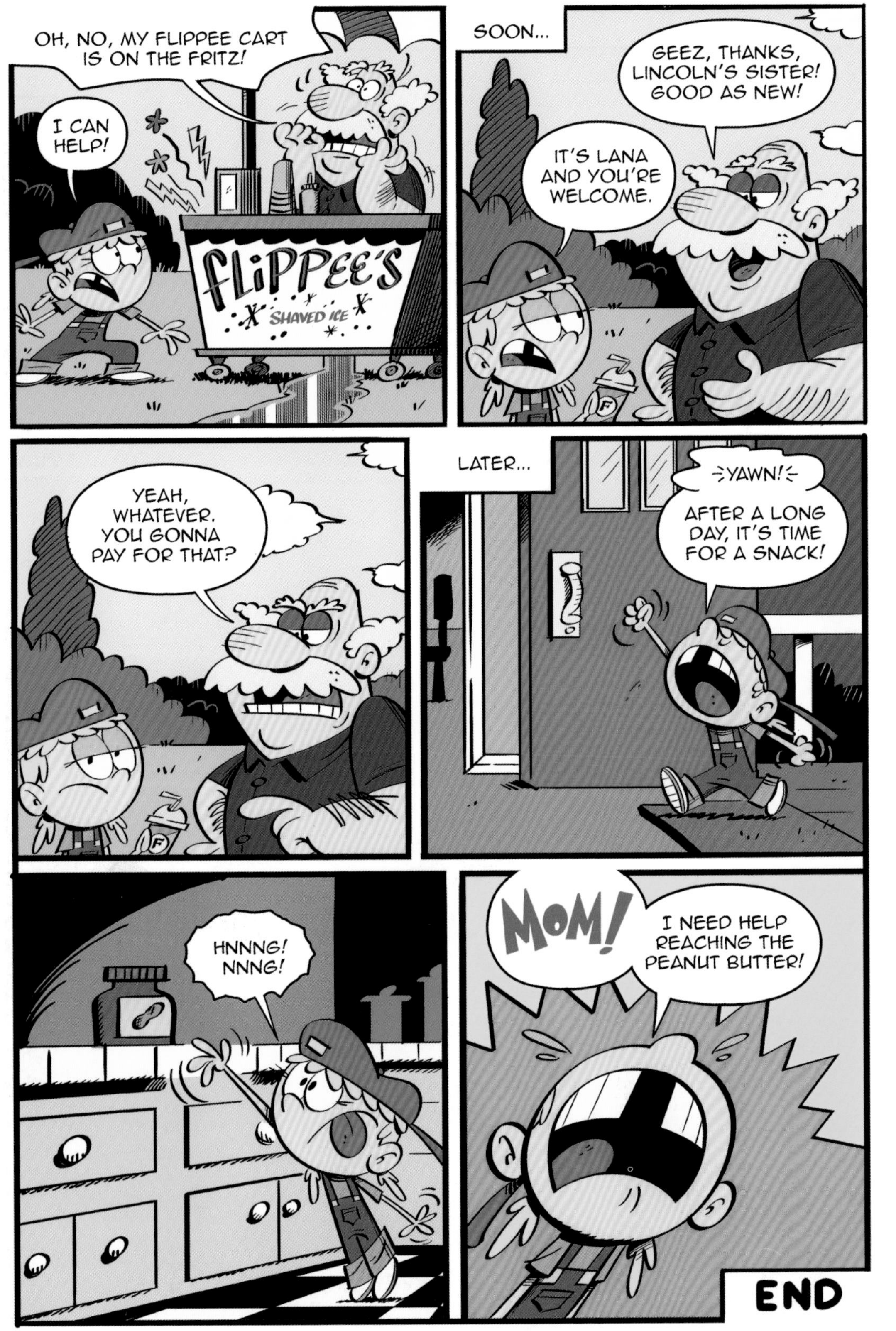
OH, NO, MY FLIPPEE CART IS ON THE FRITZ!
I CAN HELP!
FLIPPEE'S
SHAVED ICE
SOON...
GEEZ, THANKS, LINCOLN'S SISTER! GOOD AS NEW!
IT'S LANA AND YOU'RE WELCOME.
YEAH, WHATEVER. YOU GONNA PAY FOR THAT?
LATER...
YAWN!
AFTER A LONG DAY, IT'S TIME FOR A SNACK!
HNNNG! NNNG!
MOM!
I NEED HELP REACHING THE PEANUT BUTTER!
END

"ABCs OF GETTING THE LAST SLICE"

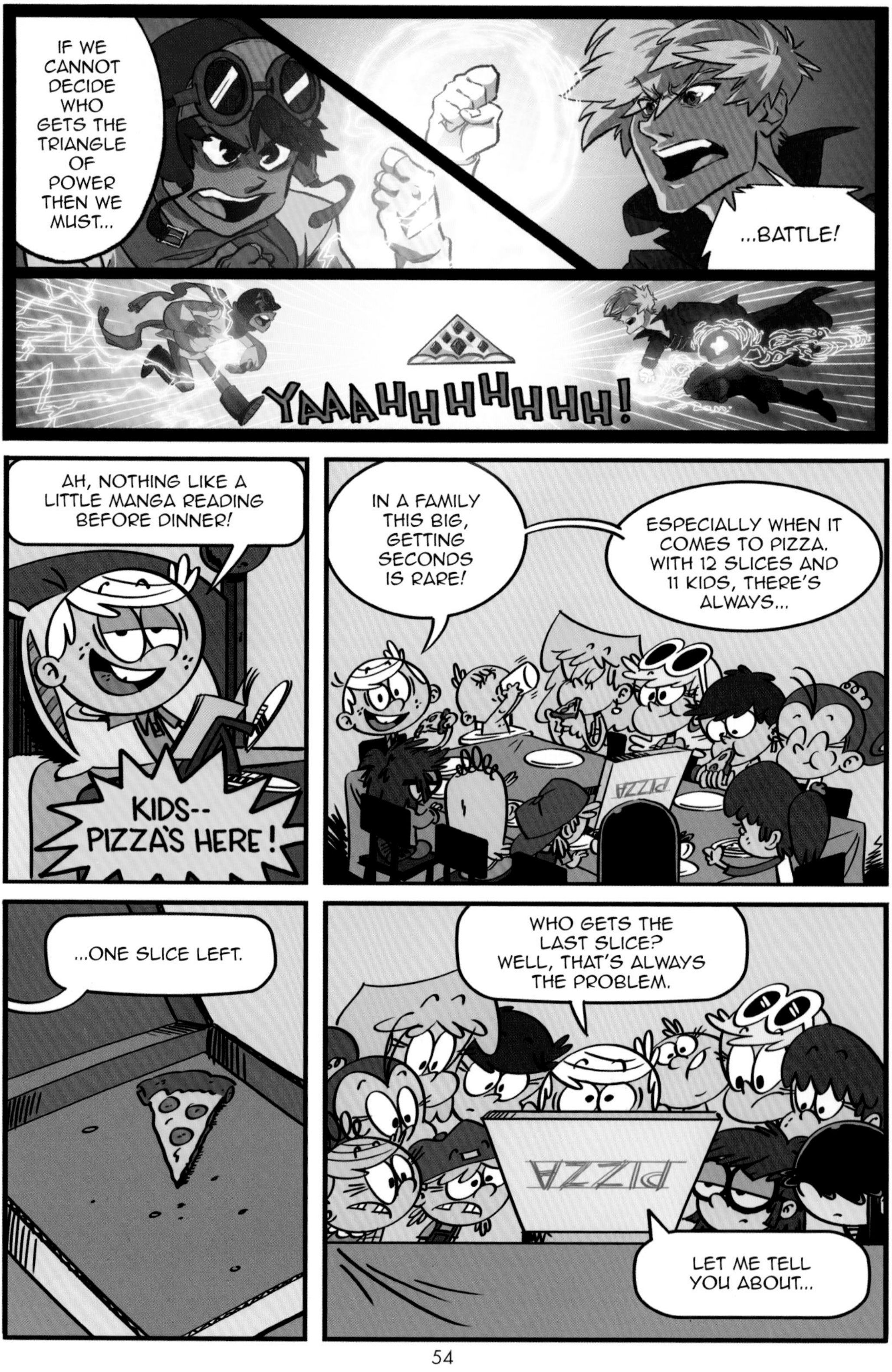
IF WE CANNOT DECIDE WHO GETS THE TRIANGLE OF POWER THEN WE MUST...
...BATTLE!
YAAAHHHHHHHHH!
AH, NOTHING LIKE A LITTLE MANGA READING BEFORE DINNER!
KIDS-- PIZZA'S HERE!
IN A FAMILY THIS BIG, GETTING SECONDS IS RARE!
ESPECIALLY WHEN IT COMES TO PIZZA. WITH 12 SLICES AND 11 KIDS, THERE'S ALWAYS...
PIZZA
...ONE SLICE LEFT.
WHO GETS THE LAST SLICE? WELL, THAT'S ALWAYS THE PROBLEM.
PIZZA
LET ME TELL YOU ABOUT...

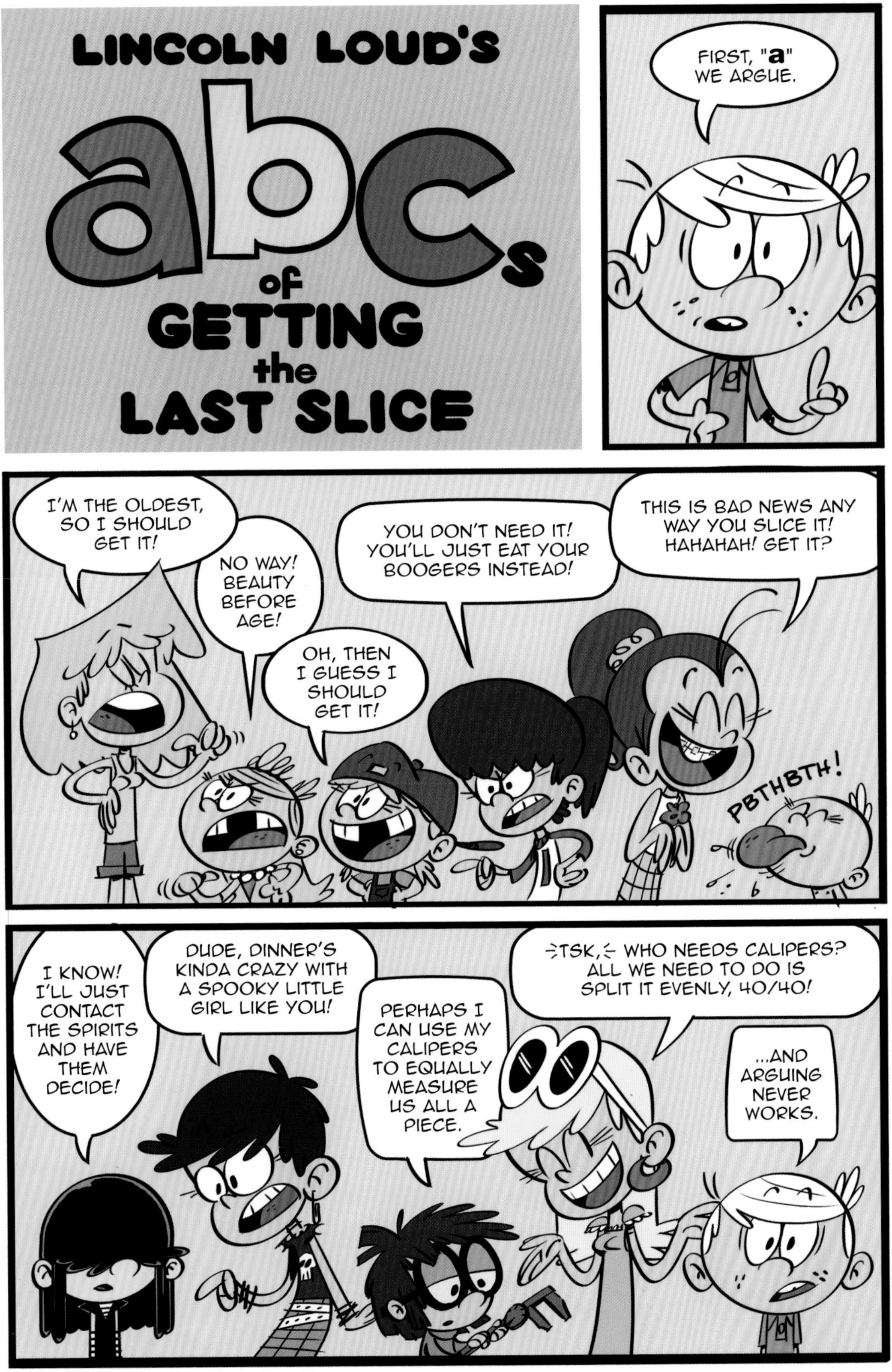
LINCOLN LOUD'S
abcs
of
GETTING
the
LAST SLICE
FIRST, "a" WE ARGUE.
I'M THE OLDEST, SO I SHOULD GET IT!
NO WAY! BEAUTY BEFORE AGE!
OH, THEN I GUESS I SHOULD GET IT!
YOU DON'T NEED IT! YOU'LL JUST EAT YOUR BOOGERS INSTEAD!
THIS IS BAD NEWS ANY WAY YOU SLICE IT! HAHAHAH! GET IT?
PBTHBTH!
I KNOW! I'LL JUST CONTACT THE SPIRITS AND HAVE THEM DECIDE!
DUDE, DINNER'S KINDA CRAZY WITH A SPOOKY LITTLE GIRL LIKE YOU!
PERHAPS I CAN USE MY CALIPERS TO EQUALLY MEASURE US ALL A PIECE.
TSK, WHO NEEDS CALIPERS? ALL WE NEED TO DO IS SPLIT IT EVENLY, 40/40!
...AND ARGUING NEVER WORKS.

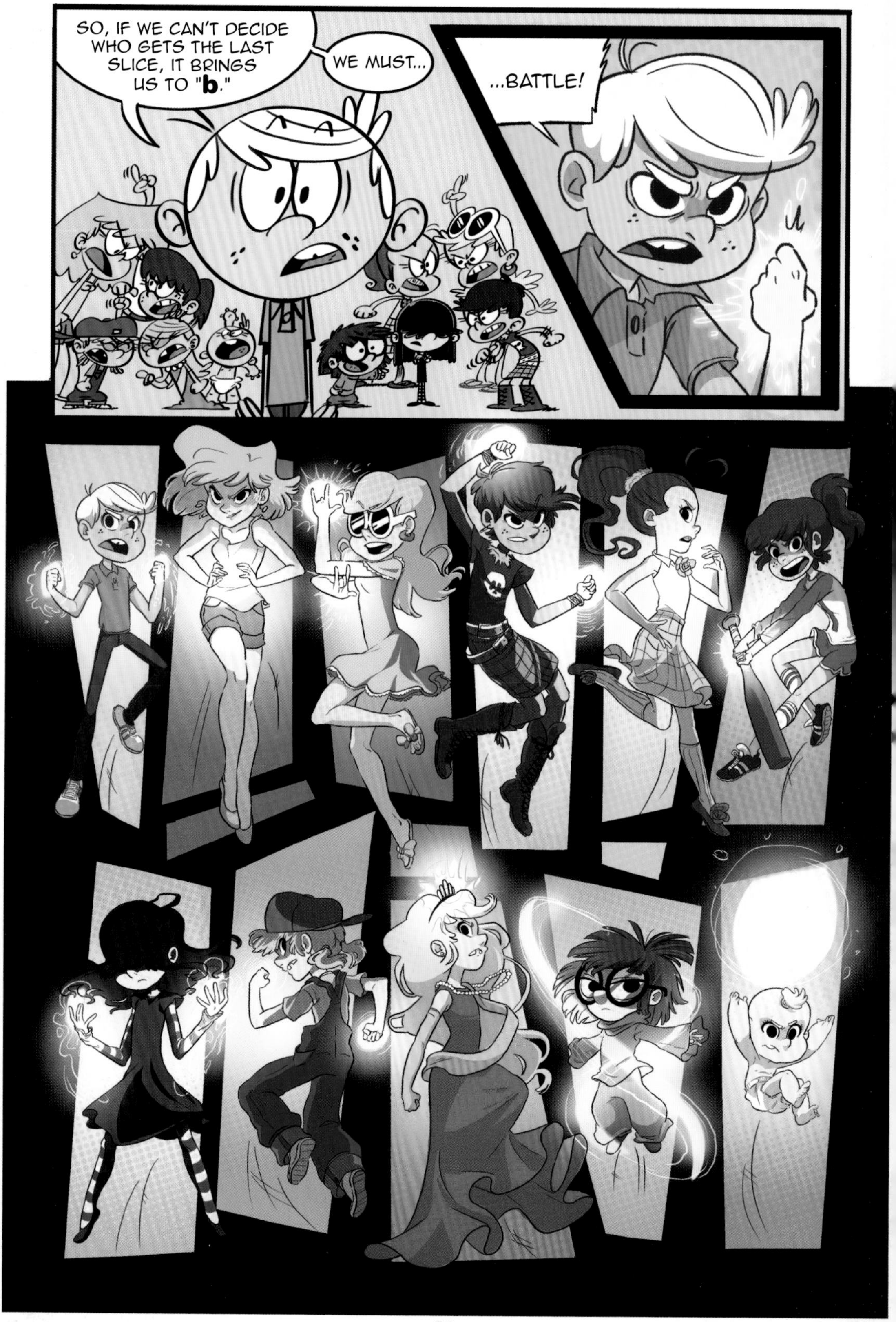
SO, IF WE CAN'T DECIDE WHO GETS THE LAST SLICE, IT BRINGS US TO "b."
WE MUST...
...BATTLE!

YAAAHHHHHHHH!

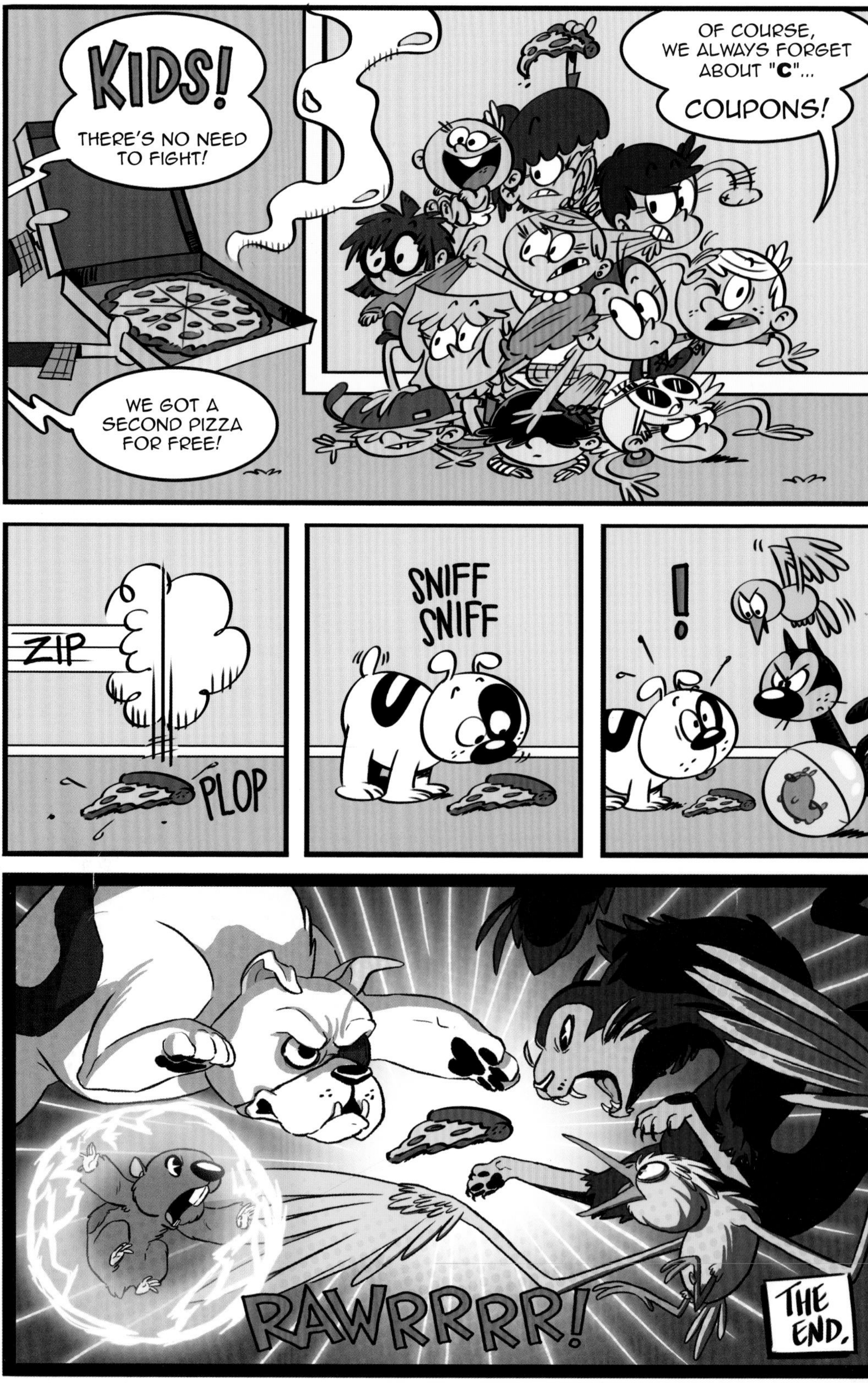
KIDS!
THERE'S NO NEED TO FIGHT!
WE GOT A SECOND PIZZA FOR FREE!
OF COURSE, WE ALWAYS FORGET ABOUT "C"...
COUPONS!
ZIP
PLOP
SNIFF SNIFF
!
RAWRRRRR!
THE END.

"BEDTIME STORIES"

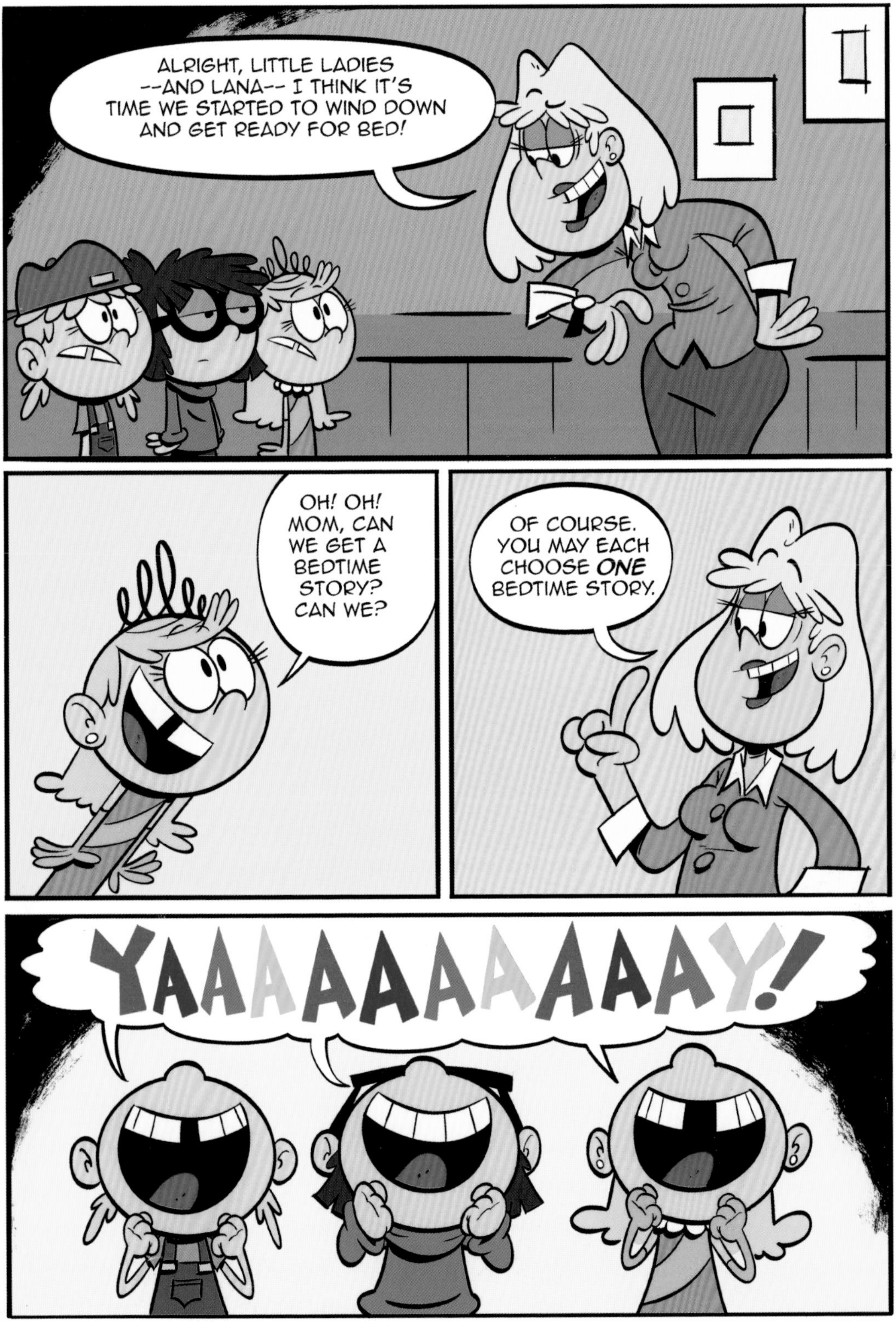

ALRIGHT, LITTLE LADIES --AND LANA-- I THINK IT'S TIME WE STARTED TO WIND DOWN AND GET READY FOR BED!
OH! OH! MOM, CAN WE GET A BEDTIME STORY? CAN WE?
OF COURSE. YOU MAY EACH CHOOSE *ONE* BEDTIME STORY.
YAAAAAAAAAY!

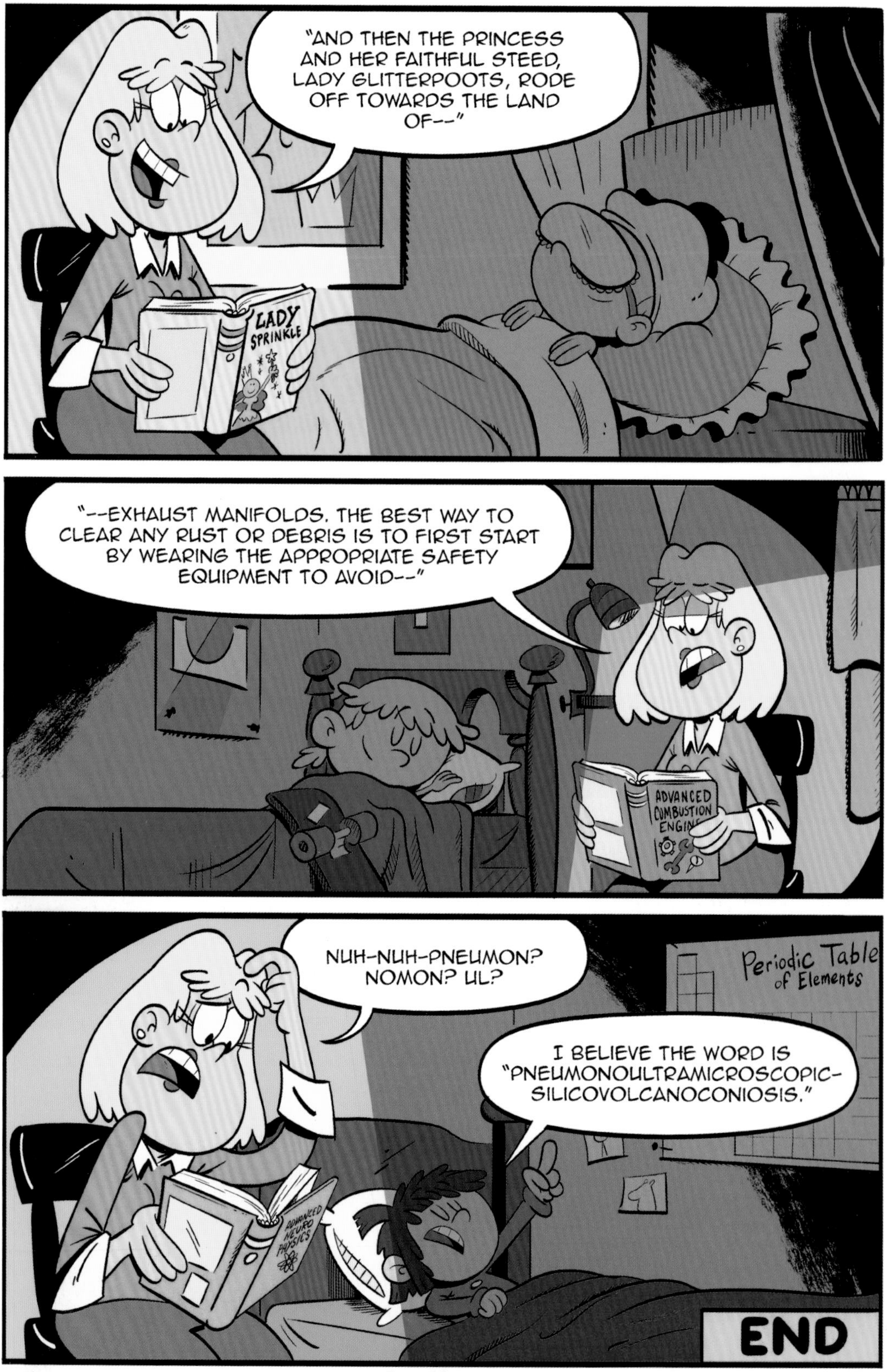
"AND THEN THE PRINCESS AND HER FAITHFUL STEED, LADY GLITTERPOOTS, RODE OFF TOWARDS THE LAND OF--"
LADY SPRINKLE
"--EXHAUST MANIFOLDS. THE BEST WAY TO CLEAR ANY RUST OR DEBRIS IS TO FIRST START BY WEARING THE APPROPRIATE SAFETY EQUIPMENT TO AVOID--"
ADVANCED COMBUSTION ENGIN
NUH-NUH-PNEUMON? NOMON? UL?
Periodic Table of Elements
I BELIEVE THE WORD IS "PNEUMONOULTRAMICROSCOPIC-SILICOVOLCANOCONIOSIS."
ADVANCED NEURO PHYSICS
END

WATCH OUT FOR PAPERCUTZ ™

Welcome to the third THE LOUD HOUSE graphic novel from Papercutz—those child-like folks dedicated to publishing great graphic novels for all ages. I'm Jim Salicrup, the Editor-in-Chief and non-stop Nickelodeon viewer, here with a different type of announcement than usual…

Usually, I'd try to draw your attention to the other Nickelodeon graphic novels from Papercutz. I'd point out that there are THE LOUD HOUSE comics in the NICKELODEON PANDEMONIUM! graphic novels, as well as comics featuring BREADWINNERS, HARVEY BEAKS, PIG GOAT BANANA CRICKET, and SANJAY AND CRAIG. I might even offer up a quick, snappy description of each series. For instance: *BREADWINNERS are SwaySway and Buhdeuce, two quazy ducks who fly around in a super sweet rocket van, delivering bread to hungry beaks everywhere on the planet Pondgea! HARVEY BEAKS is the story of the unlikely friendship between a kid who's never broken the rules and his two friends who've never lived by any! PIG GOAT BANANA CRICKET—Four best friends having the time of their lives in a weird and wild city where absolutely anything goes! SANJAY AND CRAIG follows the epic, hilarious adventures of Sanjay, a twelve year old boy who proves the old adage: there's nothing you can't accomplish (or destroy) as long as your best friend is a talking snake!* But you probably know all about these great shows already, and know that the Nickelodeon graphic novels from Papercutz feature all-new stories starring all of these awesome characters.

Or maybe I'd make a point of mentioning how appreciative we are to work with many of the artists and writers of THE LOUD HOUSE animation crew in creating the all-new stories and comics for THE LOUD HOUSE graphic novel series. After all, who better to capture the style and feel of the show than the folks who actually write and animate THE LOUD HOUSE?

Or I'd mention that one of the great plusses of the multi-story format of THE LOUD HOUSE graphic novels is that we're able to spotlight certain characters in stories of their own. For example, we feature a couple of stories starring members of the Casagrande family as part of the mix, this time around.

The announcement I have to make is especially fitting to present in a graphic novel that's all about families. And I believe it's the first time we've ever made such an announcement in a Papercutz graphic novel. It's a birth announcement! Whitney Wetta, the writer of "A Pirate's Life for CJ," "Clowning Problems," "Babes in the City" (with Sammie Crowley), and "Share Bears," is proud to announce the birth of Maxwell Maurice Wetta, born September 27, 2017. And here's a pic of Maxwell:

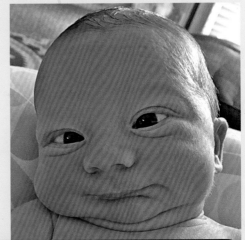

We at Papercutz congratulate proud parents Whitney and Marshall Wetta, and welcome Maxwell to the world and wish you all the very best.

When you're done aw-ing at Maxwell's pic, you may want to proceed to the preview of NICKELODEON PANDEMONIUM! #3 "Receiving you Loud and Clear," on the following pages. And don't forget to keep an eye out for THE LOUD HOUSE #4 "The Struggle is Real," coming soon. Until then, why not enjoy a Nickelodeon graphic novel with your family?

Thanks,

Jim

STAY IN TOUCH!

EMAIL: salicrup@papercutz.com
WEB: papercutz.com
TWITTER: @papercutzgn
INSTAGRAM: @papercutzgn
FACEBOOK: PAPERCUTZGRAPHICNOVELS
FANMAIL: Papercutz, 160 Broadway, Suite 700, East Wing, New York, NY 10038

Special Preview of NICKELODEON PANDEMONIUM! #3 "Receiving You Loud and Clear"

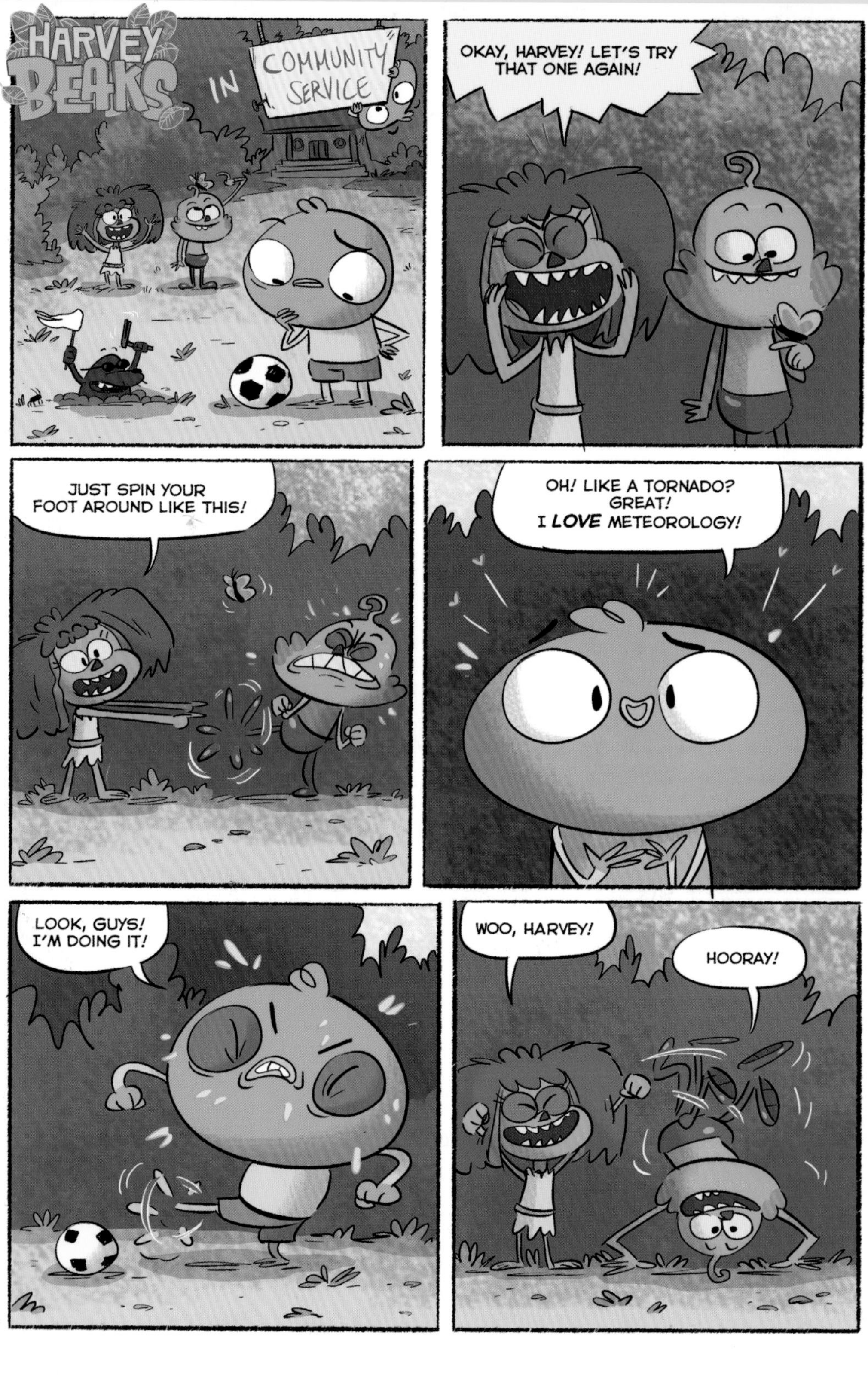
HARVEY BEAKS
IN
COMMUNITY SERVICE
OKAY, HARVEY! LET'S TRY THAT ONE AGAIN!
JUST SPIN YOUR FOOT AROUND LIKE THIS!
OH! LIKE A TORNADO? GREAT! I **LOVE** METEOROLOGY!
LOOK, GUYS! I'M DOING IT!
WOO, HARVEY!
HOORAY!

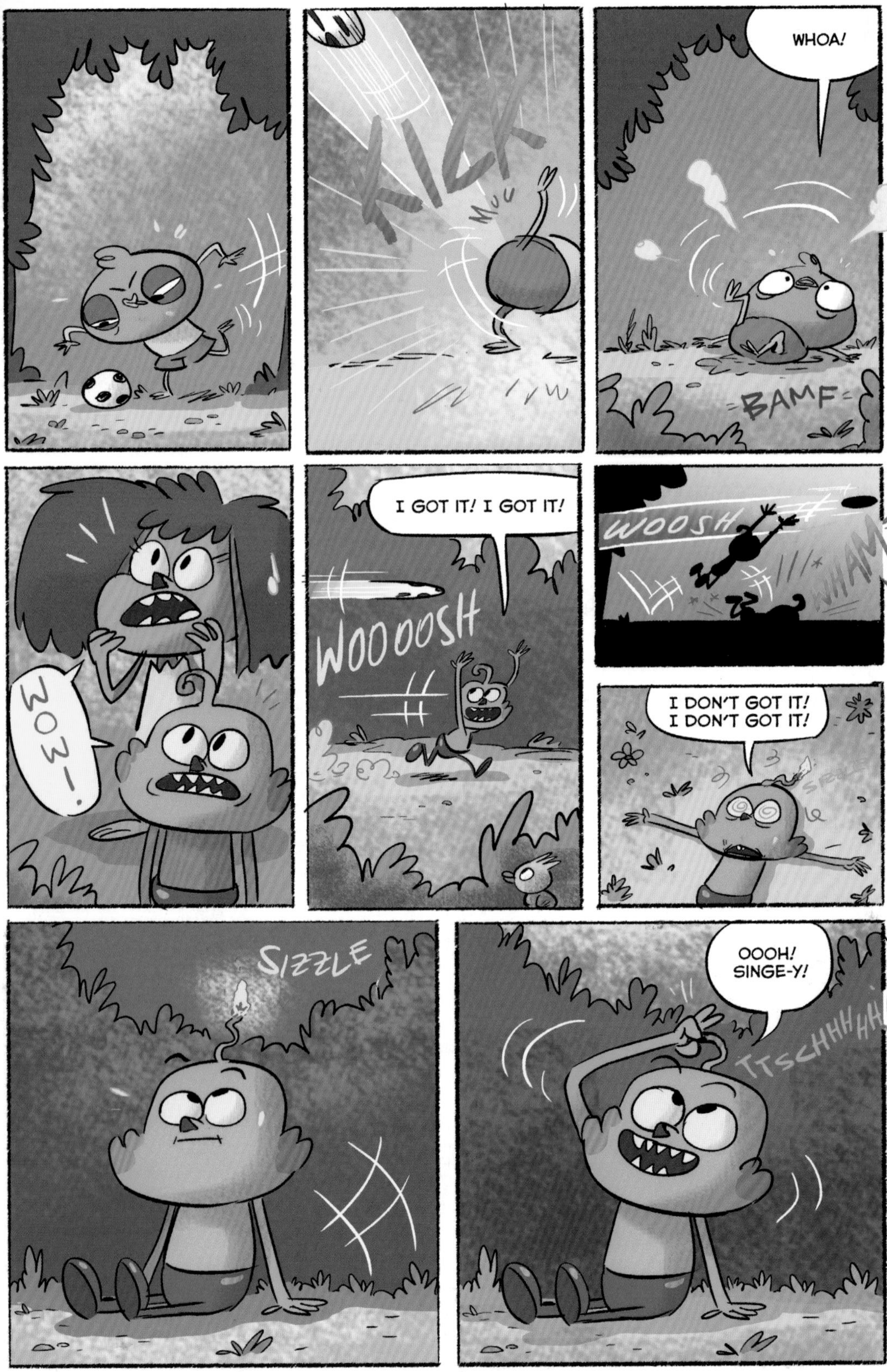
KICK
WHOA!
BAMF
WOW!
I GOT IT! I GOT IT!
WOOOOSH
WOOSH
WHAM
I DON'T GOT IT!
I DON'T GOT IT!
SIZZLE
OOOH!
SINGE-Y!
TTSCHHHHHH!

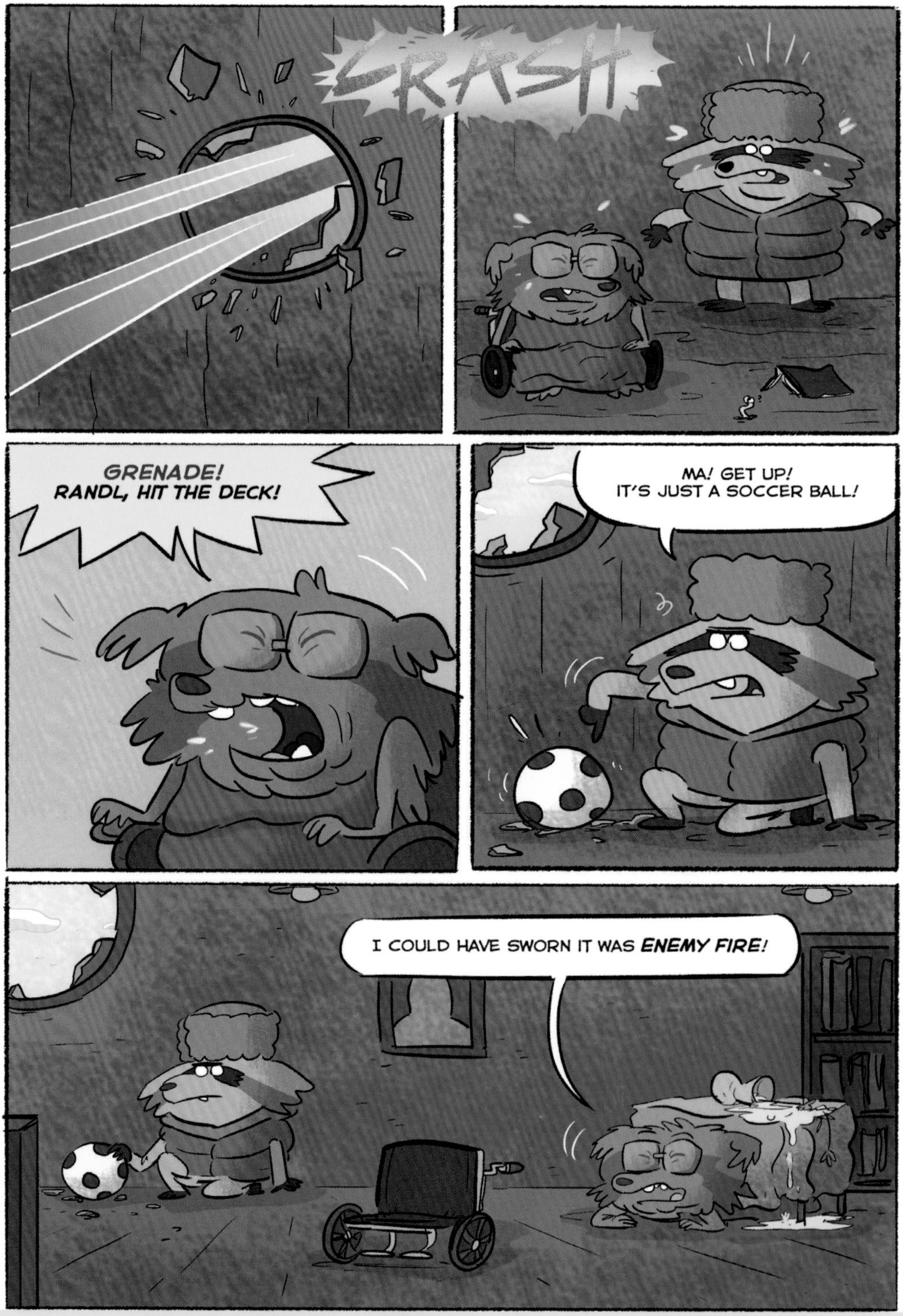
CRASH
GRENADE! RANDL, HIT THE DECK!
MA! GET UP! IT'S JUST A SOCCER BALL!
I COULD HAVE SWORN IT WAS ENEMY FIRE!

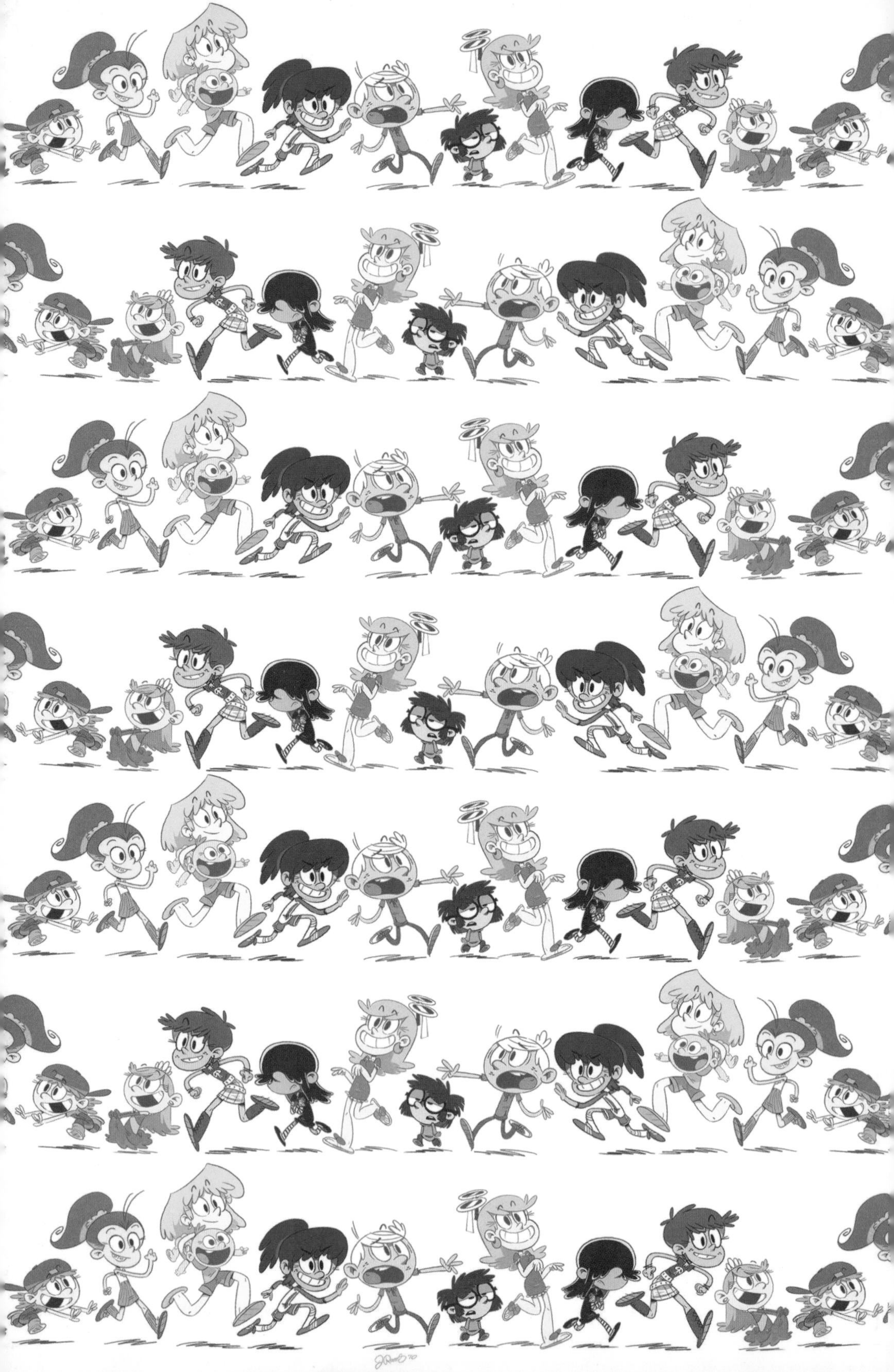